I would like to dedicate my first novel to my father, Joe Harrison, who was an author himself and told me, encouragingly, that he liked my first story.

D0708518

David Harrison

THE RESEARCH MAN

AUSTIN MACAULEY PUBLISHERS™

LONDON • CAMBRIDGE • NEW YORK • SHARJAH

A CIP catalogue record for this title is available from the British Library.

ISBN 9781788784009 (Paperback)
ISBN 9781788784016 (Hardback)
ISBN 9781788784023 (E-Book)

www.austinmacauley.com

First Published (2018)
Austin Macauley Publishers Ltd™
25 Canada Square
Canary Wharf
London
E14 5LQ

I would like to thank my wife for diligently word-processing the first few chapters until I finally got my Dragon software. Thanks also to my friends and colleagues who read the script and encouraged me to get it published.

Chapter 1
The Institute

Peter leaned back in his chair as he watched the tennis players. He noticed the backswing, the flick of the wrist, the easy economy of movement over the court. Peter admired efficiency in everything. It was pleasant sitting in the unexpectedly warm autumn sun in Lincoln's Inn Fields, and as he lazed there he mentally went through the tasks he had to do that day.

The clock in the Inner Temple struck ten, and he walked across the road into the oak-panelled entrance hall of the Institute. He ignored the old-fashioned lift and ran up the stairs to the third floor. He was trying to keep fit, as he thought he needed the exercise, and he was delighted that his breathing rate was normal when he reached his laboratory. He was also pleased to see the 'No Smoking' sign hanging on the door. Susan beamed at him as he walked in. She was busy suturing an unconscious rat which lay on a slab in front of her, and the air was heavy with ether.

'How's it going?' he asked.

'Okay. I've done the first eighteen.'

'So you'd like some help?'

'Yes please,' she said. 'If you've got time.'

He didn't really, he had other things on his mind. Susan enjoyed his help and he quite liked working with her, but ether fumes gave him a headache.

'I'll give you a hand,' he said obligingly.

'Lovely,' she replied. 'You cut, I'll sew.'

Peter put on lab coat and gloves. He picked up the plastic anaesthesia box and opened the lid. The bottom was covered with cotton wool. He unscrewed the top of the ether bottle and dripped in some liquid. Then he picked up the next rat by the tail,

9

lowered it into the box and closed the lid. He set the timer for thirty seconds.

'One down,' he said.

'Only eighty-one to go,' added Susan encouragingly. The timer rang. Peter took the unconscious rat from the box, closed the lid carefully and placed the animal on its back on the slab. He wiped disinfectant over its left flank and its fur turned yellow. He held a portion of the rat's skin between thumb and forefinger and made a small cut with his scalpel. Some blobs of blood appeared. He slid the trocha into the cut, sliding it up and under the skin, making sure he didn't poke it into the gut cavity and then he pushed the plunger. A pellet of carcinogen was delivered under the skin and he felt with his finger to make sure it was correctly positioned.

'He's all yours,' he said.

Susan had the needle and gut ready. Two stitches. Two ties. Two snips. A quick wipe with more disinfectant and the rat was returned to its cage. The process of cancer production had begun. To study cancer you needed tumours, and to get them you either injected, fed or implanted a cancer producing chemical into animals. In about three months the implanted rats would develop cancerous growths around the pellets.

As they worked, Peter and Susan chatted. The papers were full of the assassination of President Kennedy and the shooting of his killer Oswald.

'The Russians must have had a hand in it,' said Susan. 'After all, Kennedy out-manoeuvred Kruschev. It could be revenge.'

'Can't see why they'd do it,' replied Peter. 'What's in it for them? All they've done is provoke a right-wing backlash and now they've got Johnson and he hates the Commies.'

'Mm,' said Susan. 'But I can't stop thinking about Jackie. All his brains on her skirt.'

The rat in front of her twitched, and blood dribbled from the cut. She deftly held a ball of ethered cotton-wool over its nose. The twitching stopped and she finished sewing.

'Got distracted,' she said. 'I'd better concentrate.'

They concentrated together. Peter gave her a full hour and they finished twenty-five more rats.

'You're sure you'll be all right?' he asked.

'Oh yes,' she sounded confident. 'I'll just keep going. I'll stay as long as it takes.'

'Thanks, Susan. You're a star.' He hated having unfinished business. 'I'm off to see McDonald about our damned animals. It's getting urgent.'

Peter walked up to the McDonald Empire on the top floor. The chief animal technician, true to his name, was an assertive Scot who greeted Peter with an irreverent grin.

'What's up, Doc?'

Peter noted the stress on the last word. *Insult or not*, he wondered. Everyone knew his sensitivity about not being a doctor of medicine in an institute dominated by them. He decided not to rise to the bait.

'It's the rats,' he said equably. 'They were ordered months ago, and the hold-up is setting us back. Everything else is in place. So what the hell is happening?'

'I'm sorry, Dr Stott,' said McDonald. A true professional, he hated to appear wanting. 'They have been ordered, but I can't take delivery until there's room. We're full. Unless you want to buy me a new animal wing.'

'Full?' Peter was puzzled. 'You don't seem full to me. I just passed room 54 and it was almost empty.'

'Dr Lomax asked me to reserve it for him,' said McDonald, 'I don't know what he's got planned.'

'Lomax?' Peter's voice was almost shrill with disbelief. 'What does he want it for? He doesn't *do* experiments. So what's he thinking about?'

'I don't know, Dr Stott.' McDonald was getting embarrassed. 'I really don't. You'd better ask him yourself.'

'You're damn right I will.'

Peter's brain whirled as he walked downstairs. John Lomax, MD, DSc, FRCS, FIBiol, was the new Director of the Marshall Institute of Cancer Research, known in scientific circles by its acronym MICR. Lomax was a famous research scientist, but now he co-ordinated the experimental work, acquired funds and promoted the Institute. He had become, in his own woeful words, 'a bloody pen pusher'. Lomax needed no animals—he didn't even have a lab—so what was he playing at?

Back in his lab, Susan's eyes asked for help. He ignored their silent pleas, went into his office and called Dierdre Pierce, his friend and Head of Biochemistry. She too was equally baffled.

'I know less than you, Pete. We only use a few animals. You know, for an odd liver or kidney. Haven't been on the animal floor for ages. You'd better ask our superboss this afternoon.'

'I can positively guarantee it,' growled Peter. 'Damn it, we are supposed to be working together as a team. Sorry D, not getting at you.'

She laughed. 'That's okay. Reserve all your fire for our estimable director.'

The afternoon meeting was scheduled for one-thirty. This early start was due to Lomax, who arrived at eight, was hungry by noon and had eaten by one. This meant a rushed lunch for the five departmental heads, and they were not best pleased. Under the previous director, all meetings had started at a civilised half past two. New broom Lomax, recruited six months ago to reinvigorate the research programme, was already ruffling feathers.

Peter arrived early at the committee room simultaneously with Lomax's secretary. She nodded formally to him.

'Good afternoon, Doctor Stott. Dr Lomax has altered today's agenda slightly.' She handed him a piece of paper. 'Coffee?'

'Please,' said Peter. Lomax drank only the best. He glanced down at the typed sheet. It was terse and to the point.

> Executive Meeting of 27 November 1963
> Agenda
> Departmental reports
> Contracts
> Possible reorganisation
> AOB (including Thirsk)

Lomax's change was the two words after Any Other Business.

Peter was baffled again. The only Thirsk he knew was a town in Yorkshire. As he sipped his coffee, his four fellow department heads arrived. All looked tense. Dierdre Pearce sat next to Peter, pointing at the agenda and raising her eyebrows. Ron Team,

Head of Pharmacology, sat on Peter's right, gnawing his finger nails. He nodded at Peter.

'Good afternoon, colleagues.' Lomax opened the meeting exactly on time. 'Right. Reports. So, ladies first, shall we start with you, Deidre?'

All the heads had provided a written report on their progress over the past three months. All Dierdre had to do was answer any questions and amplify the report. Each head reported in turn, ensuring that everyone was up to date on the research activity in the Institute.

Next came the worrying item: contracts.

The Institute did not have a constant income. A large proportion of its money came from the Medical Research Council in the form of contracts, usually for three years. They provided money for staff, overheads, chemicals and the like. Fifteen contracts were due to terminate next April, and so to keep the research going it was essential to get some more, preferably those with big money attached. They would not be officially awarded until the New Year, but Lomax had excellent contacts in the research world and knew everything that was going on.

'Right. Contracts,' he said. 'I've had my nose really close to the ground over this. What with all the government economies.' He sighed, as if the world's problems rested totally on his shoulders. 'As far as I've found out we've not done well. Not as badly as we could have, but we *have* lost out. As far as I know we will be getting nine new contacts, all pretty much the same in terms of money. So, to the hard reality. Each department gets two, except you, Ron. You've just the one. I'm truly sorry. It's really cruel, in view of all your hard work.'

'Hell fire,' muttered Team. 'Hell bloody fire.'

The department heads knew exactly why he was cursing. Two lucrative contracts were being cut and replaced by one with minimal financial resources. We were all genuinely sorry for Team, a conscientious and effective researcher who had had a run of bad luck. They commiserated with him, and the meeting dissolved into a discussion of the inequities of the research council's decision. Peter was privately elated, his department had got away relatively unscathed, but there was still the next item on the agenda. Reorganisation.

As some departments had been hit hard, Lomax might suggest a redistribution of the permanent staff. It had happened in the past, when he lost two of his best technicians, and Peter had not forgotten the insult. He was preparing to fight his corner when Lomax called the meeting to order.

'Right, colleagues, we have had our discussion. Could we return to the agenda, please? I have had a change of plan. I propose to delay any discussion on reorganisation until a later date. We really *cannot* discuss it until we have the final contracts in front of us.'

It was a cop-out and all the heads knew it. The chances of Lomax getting it wrong were remote.

'That leaves only AOB,' continued Lomax. 'If you've no objections, I'll go first. This is only a tentative and informal look see to see how you all feel. I imagine to some of you it will all be highly contentious. Sorry, I'm getting dry.' He poured himself a second cup of coffee.

'I wish he'd get on with it,' mouthed Dierdre to Peter.

'Right,' continued Lomax. 'Thirsk. Thirsk Investments. They are a venture capital company anxious to get into the pharmaceutical world. They are seriously considering buying up the patent rights for cytocide with a view to marketing it. Some of you will know that cytocide has had a variable track record.' He sighed. 'Some tests have shown striking effects against cancer cells in-vitro and against some carcinomas in animals. An equal number of tests have shown little anti-cancer activity. One striking thing about it all is the consistency of the inconsistency, if you see what I mean. But, when it works, cytocide seems effective, and a potential money maker.' He paused. 'So, to the point. Thirsk will take up the patent if they know that (a) cytocide is a true bill and (b) have an explanation as to why some of the tests were negative. That's where we come in. Thirsk wants us to test the drug. For a fee, a very high fee. That's it in a nutshell.'

There was a long incredulous silence, broken by Deirdre.

'I don't like this at all,' she said. Peter had never heard such edge in her voice. 'Not a bit. MICR is a research institute, pure and simple, it always has been. It's not a testing station.' She glanced at Peter. 'Anyway, we don't have enough animal facilities. Why on earth don't Thirsk get it tested commercially in the usual way?'

Lomax was unruffled. 'Sorry, I forgot to mention the animals. Thirsk's money will allow us to rent or buy suitable accommodation for them. We've identified a suitable place in Clerkenwell that would fit the bill. But what they are really buying is our expertise and world reputation. If we say cytocide is okay they'll have enough to take up the patent. I know this is difficult, I know it goes against your scientific Puritanism, but it *is* a way forward. It will only be a one-off and it will ease us through any financial crisis. In my heart of hearts I think it's the right thing to do.'

The expressions on their faces told him that some thought otherwise. He decided on a strategic withdrawal.

'I've summarised my proposals here,' he said, indicating a pile of papers. 'It's all there, with detailed staff and financial considerations. I intend to propose the matter as a *formal* agenda item at our next meeting, and I would hope for your support. I'm available any time tomorrow if any of you want to discuss it. Now, please excuse me, I have another meeting to go to.'

With that he rose and left, followed by his secretary.

Peter mechanically poured himself another coffee. Dierdre did likewise, her face pale.

'Damn it, Peter, what have we got here? What the hell is he playing at? God? First that business over the contracts. Dishing them out like candy to kids, not even telling Team the results in advance. Even worse, we've got to become a damn testing station. Over my dead body. Hell, Peter, we're scientists, not puppets. Lomax is a scientist too, at least I thought he was.' She paused, adding venom to her voice. 'And to think I actually *wanted* him as Director.'

'I wanted him too.' Peter was both soothing and feigning pragmatism. 'Lomax is no fool, he's playing a long game.' He glanced down at the financial summary. 'Look at that. He's obviously worked hard on Thirsk to get that sort of money and he obviously thinks that it will persuade us. Damn it, he's so sure of us that he's even reserved a room for the animals.' He paused. 'And you know, D, he might just be on the right track.'

'Not in my book,' she snapped, and went over to commiserate with Ron Team.

Susan was still busy with the rats when Peter got back to the lab. She opened her mouth to speak, saw his face, and said nothing. Peter donned a lab coat and gloves and silently resumed the stitching. The rat supply finally ran out and Susan put the last rat into its cage. She carefully stacked all the cages on the trolley and prepared to move them back to their home on the fifth floor. It was only then that Peter remembered his manners.

'Thank you so much, Susan.' He patted her on the back, not noticing her smile. 'You've worked like a dog. Sorry for the bad company. It was a hell of a meeting.'

'I could see it was rough.' She smiled directly at him. 'Are you off now?'

'No, I'll wait. I'll see you to the station.'

They walked companionably across the park and up to Holborn tube station. After goodbyes Susan went east to Ilford and Peter went west. At Paddington he just grabbed the fast train to Maidenhead and stood all the way. Finally it was just a short bike ride to the house where he was raised, the house with its garden down to the misty Thames where he hoped Anne would have the supper ready. Normally she was in the kitchen dressed in her artist's smock, but today she was in the dining room looking stunning in her best blue dress. It showed off the colour of her eyes.

'Is this a special day?' he asked guiltily, wondering if he'd forgotten an important date.

'I hope so,' she replied. 'I've got some news for you.'

'And I you.'

'So tell me,' she said.

'No, ladies first.'

Anne pirouetted on her heels, swishing her skirt and showing off her excellent legs. She sang as she twirled.

'Yo ho, daddy O. Yo ho, daddy O.'

Peter looked blank.

'Where's the brains?' she mocked cheerfully. 'Where's the perception of my scientist husband?'

She twirled again, poking him in the ribs.

'Yo ho, daddy O *to be*.'

The penny dropped, as did Peter's jaw.

'You mean? Really? *Really*? But I thought you'd said we'd wait?'

''Tis a woman's privilege to change her mind.'

'Wow!' he said. 'Wow! Come *here.*' With a rare moment of complete abandon he grasped her by the waist and swung her around in pure delight.

'Put me down,' she giggled delightedly. 'I'm in *such* a delicate condition.'

The rest of the evening passed in a whirl. Good food, good wine. Peter sent a telegram to his mother-in-law who didn't have a phone, and whom he knew would be delighted to be a grandmother. Then an early night with some excellent congratulatory sex. As they lay together afterwards, Anne poked him.

'So, daddy dear, what do you want it to be?'

'I think I want a boy,' said Peter.

'So do I.' Anne gave him a kiss. 'I'm going to remember this evening forever.'

'I'll remember the whole day,' said Peter cautiously.

'Oh yes, sorry, I should have asked about your news.'

'Nothing as important as yours,' said her husband. 'Just Lomax making waves. Nothing we can't handle.'

'Good,' said Anne. 'Night, darling.'

She curled up like a cat and went instantly to sleep, while Peter lay awake for hours, thinking about his unborn son.

And Lomax.

Chapter 2
Battle Lines

Anne was still asleep when Peter awoke. Her hair on the pillow framed her face and Peter thought she looked just like a Madonna. He kissed her lightly, slipped out of bed, and in slippers and dressing gown went down to the kitchen. The clock stared at him accusingly. Half past eight. God, he hadn't set the alarm.

He phoned the Institute. The receptionist answered and put him through to the lab. No reply. She cut in again. Peter asked if he could leave a message. Yes, he could. And yes, Dr Lomax was in, he'd just arrived with Dr Team.

Peter decided that if he was going to be late he might as well enjoy it. He warmed some milk and took it up to Anne. She stirred in protest, so he put the glass on the bedside table and left. Downstairs he filled another glass with orange juice, took out an old blanket from the chest and went out into the garden. At the river he put the blanket on the damp bench, sat down and gazed around. The sun slanted through the mist, burnishing the trees and the water, and a fish rose leisurely, sending steel-pink ripples into the encircling steam. Peter and his father had always thought that only a Monet or a Whistler could do justice to the scene, but Anne had come close. The Impressionist oil she had done that summer had pride of place in their living room, and there was a close copy of it in the gallery in Marlow.

The garden was the last place that Peter had had a meaningful conversation with his father. They both loved fishing, and that evening his father had hooked a huge perch. He was so weak that Peter had to reel it in, but his father's enthusiasm was unabated.

'That's it then. One of the best I've ever caught. That's the way to go out. On a high.'

He went out a week later, in the room now occupied by his son and daughter-in-law.

His river garden was Peter's favourite spot. He had swum there, camped there, and climbed every tree. Aged fourteen he had revised his geometry theorems there on the seat, and it was there, four years later, that he had excitedly opened the letter from Oxford, offering him a place at New College. The garden was a place for reflection and renewal, a place where the guilt and pleasures of the past formed a continuum into the present and future. Peter was thinking of his unborn son, who might be a fisherman, and was smiling at the thought of teaching him fishing when he felt Anne's hand on his shoulder.

'Hello, darling,' she said. 'Isn't it gorgeous? And they said it was going to rain. Thanks for the milk.' She rubbed his cheek. 'God, you're rough. And cold. You'd better come in before you catch your death.'

'That's what I said to Dad,' said Peter bitterly. 'On the day he caught the perch. He just laughed. "Bring it on", he said.'

Anne patted him. 'Come on. You need a hot coffee. And a shave. And breakfast. In that order.'

The clean shaven Peter arrived at the Institute at half past eleven. Susan, as usual, was pleased to see him.

'I thought you might not be coming in,' she said. 'I thought you might be ill.'

'Didn't you get my message?'

'No,' she replied. 'Nothing at all.'

Peter made a mental note to rocket that receptionist.

'I sent one,' he said. 'Anyway, what's new? Are the rats okay?'

'Oh, yes. They're buzzing about like bees, and no casualties,' she said proudly. 'Oh, I nearly forgot. Dr Team wants to see you. He's been up twice looking for you.'

'Then I'd better go and see him.'

Team's office was on the second floor at the front, overlooking the park where the autumn breeze chased leaves into circles. The room was immaculately tidy, with none of the clutter of the usual researcher. Team sat in his arm chair, gazing out of the window and chewing a pencil. He was a tall man, with an ascetic look which reminded Peter of Sherlock Holmes. Women saw him as striking rather than handsome, and he wore his age well, with few crow's feet and a full head of hair. He relaxed when he saw Peter.

'Nice to see you,' he said, pointing to a chair. 'Thanks for coming down. We thought you weren't coming in.'

'I couldn't stay away after yesterday's antics,' said Peter. 'I was just late. Too much celebrating last night.'

'Celebrating?' Team was amazed.

'Yes. Anne's pregnant.'

Team's tired face lit up with enthusiasm. 'Well done, congratulations! So you're both well pleased?'

'Oh yes,' said Peter. 'I've really not taken it in yet. And yes, you're right, we're both delighted. But that's not why you asked me down.'

'You're right, it isn't. I really wanted to see where you are in all of this. We're having an impromptu meeting of the Heads at half past twelve.'

'Are we?' Peter railed at being the last to be told.

'Sorry, Peter. But as I said we thought you weren't coming in.'

'I'll crucify that receptionist,' said Peter. 'Anyway, enough of that, what are your thoughts? You seemed absolutely shattered yesterday.'

'I was.' Team was opening up to his younger friend. 'I was simply appalled. It wasn't the testing thing, I can live with that— it's just a stopgap. Not very professional, but expedient. It was the cancellations. I've never had anything like them before. Every other time the MRC always gave me the benefit of the doubt, so to speak. Look at my track record. You know about viromycin?'

'Yes,' replied Peter. 'But not in detail.' Actually he did, but he wanted Team to expand, which his colleague did in full lecturer mode.

'It's just that we can't get enough of it,' continued Team. 'Viromycin, I mean. It's produced in tiny amounts by cells in response to viral attack. So it should have huge anti-viral properties—and could work against virally induced cancers. Its potential is colossal. But the amounts we can extract are tiny. Minute. And we can't get it pure enough. So the results are inconsistent, but promising. In the past the MRC would have given me time to see if it's a real bill. But not now. They've cancelled it, and I don't see why.'

'I really am sorry,' said Peter. He meant every word. 'You've had six years on it. It *is* six, isn't it? And as you say, the potential is absolutely enormous.'

'You're right,' replied Team. 'And they must know that. So why can't they see it through? It's as if they've taken against me. Oddly enough, that's made me in favour of the testing. At least we'll be able to see if one thing actually works.'

Peter sat silently, carefully selecting his words.

'I can't think they've taken against you, Ron. Why should they? I sometimes think I'm paranoid but I've never obsessed about the Medical Research Council. They've always been absolutely straight. But, if you really *do* want to know, you could check out if all the contracts for viromycin were cancelled. If they weren't, then MRC is anti-you. If they're all cancelled, they've given up on viromycin. But do you really want to know?'

Team sat back, contemplating.

'You're right, Peter. Do I really want to know? On par I think I do. At least it will give my brain a rest. And let me get a good night's sleep.'

'I didn't sleep much last night either,' empathised Peter. 'But that was different. Anyway, back to the testing. You're obviously very much in favour of it. I'm a bit more cautious, but overall I think I'm backing it. It should tide us over the hard times.'

'Good,' said Team. He beamed and shook Peter's hand. 'That's two of us for, only three more to convince. Nice to have you on board, Peter. And thanks. See you at the meeting.'

So that's it, thought Peter as he ran upstairs. *Lomax's roped in Team and he thinks he's got me. So it's three for, three against.*

The battle lines were being drawn.

Back in the lab, Peter started rechecking some of his past results. He had to give a talk on cancer induction at the Biochemical Society meeting in Cambridge in two weeks' time, and needed to get the slides prepared. The huge clatter of his mechanical calculator drowned out Susan's conversation with another technician, but when the machine stopped, Susan's voice cut in. 'We saw a really good film last night. Actually it was a

Western, and normally I don't like them, but John asked me out and so I went. It's called "Ride the High Country". It was so sad, I cried at the end when the hero was killed.'

'So who was the hero?'

'An actor called Joel McCrea,' replied Susan. 'I've never seen him before. Apparently, he was a big star in the forties. John thought he was really good, and so did I. To me he looked just like Doctor Lomax, very handsome, lovely silver hair.'

That name was enough for Peter.

'So who's this film critic?' he snapped. 'This John. A new boyfriend?'

'Oh no, Doctor Stott,' said Susan. 'He's just a friend. I've known him for years. *Not* a boyfriend.'

'Really?' said Peter sarcastically. 'Anyway, enough of that. I'm off to a meeting of the Heads.' He stopped. 'And I'm *sure* we *won't* be discussing Doctor Lomax's good looks.'

Susan gaped at the *lèse-majesté.*

Same committee room. Different time and day. As Peter walked in, he saw the chair occupied by Lomax the previous day was now filled by Stephens, Head of Medicine.

'Come in, Peter,' he said grandly. 'Now we are five.'

Peter sat down and looked around. Team smiled at him. Dierdre averted her eyes. Next to Stephens sat Paul Ince, the head of Histology and Cell Biology. He waved genially.

Stephens opened the proceedings.

'This is becoming something of a habit,' he said. 'Our second unofficial meeting in four months. I'm not chairing the meeting, I'm just the facilitator. I thought we'd just go round the table and see how everybody feels. For me the money is more than okay. So that leaves two questions. Do we go for testing, and if so, who will do it? You start, Dierdre.'

Peter knew exactly what Doctor Pierce was going to say. Her pedigree was immaculate. She liked pure research, would not be associated with technology and had not changed her mind overnight.

'I've said this all before,' she said. 'We do straight research. Okay, we have a financial problem. But we have our reputation, and more research will come. Ironically, it's our reputation that's getting us the testing money, and testing will be a retrograde step. I'm totally against it.'

'Ron?' asked the acting chairman.

'At first I was against it,' said Team. 'But on reflection I see no problems if the testing is a one-off. No one is really suggesting anything else.'

'Not yet,' spat Dierdre.

The next to speak was Ince. In the Institute he did animal autopsies, tested toxins in blood, and looked at diseased cells under the microscope. Industry did not impinge on his world, and he was a man of few words who did not suffer fools gladly.

'I'm totally against it,' he said. 'The whole idea is ridiculous. Count me out. That's it in a nutshell.'

Next came Peter.

'My views are the same as Ron's,' he said. 'It's fine as a one-off until the finances are back to normal. As for who does the testing, there are only two of us who could do it. I haven't the time, so it must fall to you, Ron. Is that right?'

'I assume so,' said Team.

The other Heads exchanged glances.

Finally it was Stephen's turn. He was the most senior of the Heads and also a surgeon and, in the inverse snobbery of the surgical world, he insisted on being addressed as Mr Stephens. He tried out surgical and chemical methods against cancer in a variety of London hospitals, and though based at MICR, he spent a lot of his time at the Royal College of Surgeons just down the road. The other Heads all expected this most patrician of men to be against commerce, but he was not.

'I do testing,' he said. 'On patients. That's my job. After thinking about it, I really can't see why more testing, albeit for money, betrays our integrity. For me there's no problem if it's only a one-off and doesn't set a precedent. That's it for me. Right, now let's see if we can come up with an agreed consensus.'

His attempt at conciliation failed completely. The meeting descended into a free for all, with all the directors firmly defending their corners. After a few minutes, Peter made his excuses and left; Dierdre in full cry was a real force to be reckoned with. From the committee room he went straight to the restaurant, with its slow queue at the self-service counter. He went to the snacks section, bought a sandwich and orange juice, and retreated to a corner to reflect. So that was it, MICR would be doing contract testing, but only if he was in favour of it. Changing his mind would make the voting 3:3 and he knew that Lomax, who was new to the job, would never risk pushing through a controversial policy without a clear majority of the Heads. Neither Peter nor the previous Director had been political animals, nor had they needed to be, but with Lomax Peter realised that things had changed.

Across the restaurant the queue inched interminably towards the till, and with it went Susan. She cut a small, dainty figure, determinedly looking for a clean tray. Anne, meeting her for the first time, had described her as 'neat' and Peter realised how accurate the description was. Neatly bobbed hair, neatly pressed skirt, neat shirt waist blouse. He also realised, guiltily, how little he actually knew about her. He knew her tastes—she liked films (favourite: Gone with the Wind), Cary Grant, strong coffee, weak tea with sugar and angora sweaters, but he knew virtually nothing about her family because she always evaded any questions. He did a mental CV. Susan Preston, age 23, single, just finishing an HNC at Barking Tech, lives with widowed mother in Ilford. Eighteen words. Not much knowledge of a person who had worked with him for a year. Or was it eleven months?

Across the room Susan paid for her meal and looked round hopefully for someone to sit with. Peter took pity on her, stood up, and waved. She smiled and came across.

'Thank you for calling me over,' she said. 'I hate eating alone. Oh, I'm sorry, Doctor Stott, I didn't see you've finished.'

'That's fine,' replied Peter. 'I'll just keep you company.'

Susan carefully cut her meat into small portions while Peter chipped in with his first question.

'Susan, how long have you worked with me?'

'Ten months and two weeks,' she answered promptly. She took her first mouthful.

'And you're happy at the Institute?'

'Oh yes, Doctor Stott, I love it.'

Peter was getting increasingly irritated at being addressed as Dr Stott. It was an unwritten rule at the Institute that Heads of departments were always addressed formally, and Director Lomax had enforced that policy, but Peter was feeling rebellious.

'Then I think if you're going to stay on with me, you should call me Peter. You can't keep on with this Doctor Stott habit.'

Susan blushed. 'If you want me to. Of course I will. Thank you, Doctor St—er, Peter'

'And thank you, Miss Pres—er Susan.'

They both laughed, and Susan relaxed.

'Your dinner's getting cold,' said Peter, and Susan resumed eating. 'You know, we've got all those slides to do, and I'd like to finish them today. So I'll go up and get started. Come up when you're ready. There's no rush.'

'Yes, Peter.' Susan tried out his name and realised she wasn't blushing. 'I'll come up as soon as I can, and I'll stay till we get them done.'

'Fine,' said her boss. 'You're a star again.'

Good quality slides were essential for a good scientific presentation. Usually about ten slides were needed for a fifteen minute talk, and they had to be clearly visible to an aged professor at the back of the lecture theatre. Peter had seen some appalling slides in his career as a scientist, and was adamant that all he produced would be perfect. Susan and he had eleven to prepare, and it was a long and tedious process. They started with an oblong sheet of white cardboard. All the letters and numbers in the title were applied with a Letraset kit. Peter then ruled the faint pencil lines which outlined the columns of figures giving the results. The Letraset numbers were then applied; it was an exacting process and any mistake could mean a fresh start. Peter had finished one card when Susan arrived, and they worked on steadily together, speaking only when necessary. Then Peter started his interrogation.

'How's your mother these days?'

'Oh, she's fine.'

'Is she still working?'

'Oh, yes.'

'She's still at the shop?' As he asked the question, Peter realised he wasn't sure if it was a shop or a factory.

'No, she's not.'

The conversation died, and they concentrated on the job in hand, working steadily with regular supplements of tea. As the lab clock neared half past four, they still had two cards to finish, so Peter called Anne.

'Sorry dear, going to be late. We're finishing off the slides.'

'That's okay,' she said. 'It's fish for supper. I'll do it when you get here. So give me a time.'

'Half past seven?'

'That's fine,' she said. 'By the way, I've got some news.' She sounded agitated. 'But it'll keep. Bye darling.' The phone clicked.

Peter was concerned. After dithering a few minutes, he rang her back. There was no reply.

It took only another hour to finish off the cards, which Peter repeatedly photographed with his prized Leica.

'The deed is done,' he said proudly. 'Thanks again, Susan.'

She smiled back, putting on her coat.

'I'm ready when you are.'

It was raining steadily as they left the Institute, but in High Holborn the raindrops turned to stair rods, smashing on the pavement and filling their shoes with water. They ran desperately for shelter, Susan slipping in her heels and grabbing Peter for support. In a café doorway they wiped hair and water from their eyes, and laughed aloud at their own predicament. The door opened, and with it came the delicious aroma of ground coffee. Peter looked down at his assistant.

'Susan, I think we've earned it. How about a good espresso?'

He knew her answer before she said it.

'That would be lovely.'

She found a table by the window and Peter brought over the two coffees. They watched the rain sluice down the glass.

'What a change!' she said. 'It was so lovely in the park this morning.'

'Yes, it was the same at home,' replied Peter. 'I'm really sorry I was late, it really set us back. And you'd made an effort to get in early.'

'So had Doctor Team,' volunteered Susan. 'He doesn't usually get in before me. I followed him and Doctor Lomax across the park. That's when I thought of the Western. From behind, Doctor Team looked like Randolph Scott, and Doctor Lomax looked like Joel McRae.'

'So what were they doing?'

'Well, they weren't going in guns blazing,' giggled Susan. 'Doctor Lomax was doing a lot of talking. Doctor Team was listening—he didn't say much. He looked very down.'

'I expect Doctor Lomax was trying to cheer him up,' said Peter, doubting his words as he said them. 'Anyway, how's the coffee?'

'Lovely.'

Peter winced mentally at her favourite word.

'Thank you very much, it's a real treat.'

'No, thank you,' he said truthfully. 'It's nothing for all your hard work.'

Despite the coffee break, Peter still managed to get home on time. The dining table was laid, and there was a half wrapped haddock in the kitchen. No sign of Anne. He was about to yell out when he heard a groan, and he ran frantically upstairs. She was in the bathroom, her head in the toilet, retching. He knelt behind her, holding her shoulders, his body as tense as hers. Finally the spasm passed and she turned her white face towards him, tried to smile and answered his unspoken question.

'I'm fine. I'm not dying. Now I'm sure I'm pregnant—I've got morning sickness in the evening.'

Peter kissed her clammy forehead, got up, filled the toothbrush beaker and brought it over.

'Come on, love. Rinse your mouth out.'

She did as she was told. Then Peter unzipped her stained dress, pulled it over her head and dropped it in the bath. He half carried her into the bedroom, sat her down and pulled back the sheet.

'In you go. I'll get you a bowl and some milk. It'll take the taste away and you might be able to keep some down.'

When he returned with the warm milk, a hot water bottle and a bowl, her colour had recovered slightly.

'Thanks darling.' She sipped the milk cautiously. 'I expected it to be bad, but not as bad as this.'

'Why on earth didn't you call me?'

'It started when you rang,' she said. 'That's why I rang off so suddenly. I've been up here virtually all the time since. I did try to ring you, but all I got was the engaged signal.'

'Dear God.' Peter was aghast. 'Just you stay there, let me do the work. It's Friday today, so you can have two days of me waiting on you hand and foot.'

She laughed like the old Anne.

'There's no need. But you'll have to get your own supper. It's opening that haddock that started all this off.' Then her face fell. 'Oh, I didn't tell you. Mum's coming down—I got a telegram this morning saying she's on her way. She'll be arriving tomorrow. That's the bad news.'

'Why is it bad news?' he asked. 'It'll be nice to see her.' Peter liked his mother-in-law and she liked him, but he knew the relationship between mother and daughter was edgy.

'You know,' said Anne. 'She'll stay and stay, and I can't take that.'

'Then we'll have to keep her stay short,' replied Peter brightly, wondering as he said it how they could achieve their aim without mortally insulting his mother-in-law. 'Anyway, more to the point, where's she going to sleep?'

Anne looked guilty. 'Oh God. I haven't finished the front bedroom. It's still not cleaned and the bed's not made.' She was close to tears.

'No problem,' said Peter. 'Hubby's here. He'll do it. Get some sleep.' He tucked the eiderdown around her neck and went downstairs. There he cooked the haddock, keeping the window open to let out the smell, washed up and went upstairs. The front bedroom was Hoovered, dusted and had fresh sheets on the bed. Finally, exhausted, he went to Anne. He tossed his clothes on a chair, and crawled in beside his wife, who was sleeping peacefully. He didn't set the alarm. The night sleeper arrived at King's Cross at seven, and he knew the phone call would come just after that.

Chapter 3
Clerkenwell

Next morning, Peter waited in vain for the phone to ring, while Anne slept restlessly upstairs. At eight, the telegram boy rang the doorbell, and Peter read the message which was terse and to the point.

SORRY BAD COLD HOPE SEE YOU SAT WRITING MUM

'Any reply?' asked the boy.

'No thanks,' said Peter, handing over two shillings. The message said it all.

When Peter took up the hot milk, Anne was awake, and he handed her the telegram without speaking. To his surprise, she was really upset.

'Oh dear,' she said. 'I was so looking forward to seeing her.'

'But last night—' started Peter.

'I know,' she said. 'It wasn't that I didn't want to see her. I just didn't want her to hang on. Now I feel guilty.'

'No need,' said Peter. 'She'll be here in a week and only stay a week, so you'll have what you wanted.'

'I know.' Anne wiped the tears from her eyes. 'I suppose it's a girl thing. I'm sick and I'm pregnant and I want my Mum. Silly, isn't it? I've got you and you're looking after me, but it's Mum I'm thinking about. Seems selfish.'

'Not selfish,' said Peter. 'Just normal. So try your milk.'

For the rest of the weekend, Peter tried to find the food that Anne could keep down. Milk was okay. Milk with cornflakes was a disaster. Coffee, her favourite drink, made her retch instantly. In desperation Peter went to the local shop for ice cream. The strawberry went down well, as did strawberry milk shake.

'I'll get fat as a hog eating ice-cream,' she complained.

'You're supposed to put on weight. There's nothing wrong with a milk diet,' said Peter. 'You'll just need some iron—I'll get you some pills on Monday.'

By Sunday, Anne felt less sick and insisted on going to Marlow to hand over an oil commissioned at the amazing price of £50. The buyer was delighted.

'That Spencer thinks he's got a monopoly of Marlow paintings,' he said. 'But I like yours better. My friends will be green with envy when they see this. So you can expect some more trade.'

Anne went pink with delight. 'That's the nicest thing anyone has said about my work.'

On the way home she chatted excitedly about more commissions, forgot to look at the road and got sick. She didn't quite get the window down in time, and the result was a tiny pink stain on the carpet of her beloved MG.

Peter didn't really want to go to work on Monday, but Anne was adamant.

'You can't sit around nursing me for the next eight months,' she said firmly. 'I've just got to get on with it.'

'You're sure?'

'Of course I am. Just call me like you said.'

'Alright. And I'll come home early at four.'

'Fine. Now go.'

As Peter walked into the Institute he saw McDonald and Susan chatting by the lift.

'So, how's the king of the animals?' asked Peter.

McDonald grinned back. He liked a bit of repartee. 'I'm fine, they're fine. By the way, Dr Stott, did you find out what Dr Lomax's got planned?'

Peter looked at the animal technician. His face seemed totally guileless. He remembered Lomax's words at their last meeting. '*We have identified premises in Clerkenwell.*'

Was McDonald one of the royal 'we'? Peter wondered. He decided to try him out.

'We've discussed a future animal project,' he said truthfully. 'But it's not decided yet—it will be at the next meeting.' Then he resorted to fantasy. 'By the way, I'd forgotten to mention it. I thought I saw you or your double in Clerkenwell last week. Was that you?'

McDonald looked amazed.

'Not me,' he said. 'I live in Tottenham. Never been in Clerkenwell'

'Then you *do* have a doppelganger,' laughed Peter, and they all got into the lift.

In the lab Susan looked questioningly at her boss.

'I was just testing him,' he said.

'And did he pass?' she asked uncomprehendingly.

'Oh yes.'

He gave her no further explanation, but he now knew that Lomax had, quite unbelievably, identified animal accommodation without consulting his experienced chief animal technician.

'So are we all ready?' he asked.

'Yes, ready and waiting.'

Mondays in the oncology department were called D days. D stood for dissection, and this meant the animals on test had to be killed and fully autopsied. Peter knew that cancer could be produced using one carcinogen, such as butter yellow, which produced tumours of the liver. In a preliminary experiment rats given butter yellow and benzanthracene, another carcinogen, had died much more quickly than the rats given butter yellow alone. This implied that the presence of the second carcinogen amplified the effect of the first, a process called co-carcinogenesis. Peter knew that cigarette smoke contained several cancer causing agents and thought that co-carcinogenesis could explain its deadly effect in long-term smokers.

There were seventy rats in the experiment, divided into groups of ten. Group One were the controls; they were fed their usual diet with no carcinogens. They were alert, smooth furred and sleek. Group Two had received butter yellow in their food, and all the other groups had received butter yellow and different amounts of benzanthracene. Most looked sick, with rough fur, dull eyes and distended abdomens. Four months exposure to the cancer causing chemicals had done their work.

Susan had marshalled all their technicians and 'borrowed' one from Team's department. First came the killing. Each rat was placed on a metal mesh which it gripped with its feet. The technician then pressed scissors on the back of its neck and pulled its tail—stretching it and breaking its neck. Its throat was cut with a scalpel and the blood samples were taken. Next came the exacting task. All the organs were carefully removed and weighed. Each was examined for tumours, and if cancer was detected, a sample was kept for microscopic examination. Some tumours were obvious: the cancerous livers of the experimental rats were lumpy and grey, totally different to the smooth pink of the healthy controls.

Peter worked with a young technician, showing him the dissection technique, then handed him over to Susan. There was a quiet hum of concentrated activity in the lab, and Peter left them to it.

'I'm in the office if you need me,' he called to Susan. She smiled and nodded back.

At his desk, he rummaged for the telephone directory. It took only minutes to find and dial the number for Clerkenwell Council, where a bored receptionist put him through to the department.

'Planning. Can I help you?'

'Yes,' said Peter. 'I was wondering if you could tell me if you've had an application recently for change of use to animal facilities.'

The female voice was curt.

'We only give information on applications for which we have planning numbers. I suggest you come in and look at the files of applications. We would be glad to help you then. We are open from nine to one and two till five.' The phone clicked.

He dialled Anne. She sounded gloomy but determined.

'Still queasy, but I've kept most of my breakfast down. I'm off to the shops in a minute—I'm damned if I'll let it beat me. But do come home early.'

'As promised,' said Peter. 'With your iron pills. Look after yourself.'

'Will do. Bye darling.'

Peter went back into the lab and sat down next to Susan. She worked quietly and deftly and he felt proud of her.

'It looks good,' she said. 'With just a casual look it seems the benzanthracene is working at really low levels. The tumours are much bigger.'

'Fine,' he said. 'And what about the snaps?'

'They're being done now. Ready by Wednesday.'

'Excellent,' said her boss. 'We're on the up and up.'

Susan opened up the abdomen of another rat.

'Peter,' she said cautiously. 'Can I ask you a question?'

'Of course.'

'Jewellery. They say you know a lot about it.'

'Not a lot. Enough. Dad was a jeweller, so I got it all from him.'

'But you know more than me,' she insisted. 'It's Mum. She's very low at the moment, and it's her birthday next week. I know she'd like a real pearl and diamond ring. But it's got to be cheap.'

'Then buy it second-hand,' he said. 'Don't buy new, it's a rip-off. The best place round here is Hatton Garden.' He stopped, reflecting—Hatton Garden and Clerkenwell were very close.

'If you like,' he volunteered. 'I'll help you buy it. I'm going to Clerkenwell tomorrow, and it's just round the corner from Hatton Garden.'

'Clerkenwell?' Her eyes lit up with curiosity. '*And* Hatton Garden. At the *same* time. That would be—' she hesitated. 'Marvellous.'

'Right,' said Peter. 'We'll go after coffee and do both.'

Susan's eyes were dancing. Like Peter, she was intrigued by intrigue.

'I can't wait.'

Peter suddenly realised it was the first time ever that Susan had volunteered any information about her mother.

'Things bad at home?' he asked sympathetically.

Susan looked embarrassed.

'I'll tell you tomorrow.'

The rest of the day was taken up with finishing off the dissection and a preliminary collation of the results. Peter was delighted. The benzanthracene definitely seemed to be enhancing the growth of the liver cancer when fed at minute amounts. The tumour samples were sent to Ince's department for histological examination, the benches were scrubbed with disinfectant and the rat bodies consigned to the incinerator. By three o'clock Peter had had enough.

'Sorry, go to go.' he told Susan. 'Anne's ill.'

'Not serious, I hope.'

33

Peter didn't want to report Anne's pregnancy. 'Nothing much,' he said. 'Just a stomach upset.'

'Is it still on for tomorrow?' asked Susan anxiously. 'I'll bring the money. Twenty pounds. Do you think that'll be enough?'

'It sure as hell should be. If not, we'll grind the bastards down. I'll be in at nine as usual.'

*

It was a clear morning as Peter and Susan walked up Hatton Garden from Holborn. Susan's purse bulged with twenty hard-earned pounds. To her the jewellery area was a revelation—rows of small shops with barred windows and groups of Hassidic Jews with long hair and flat black hats. Behind the bars were treasure troves, and Peter selected one specialising in pearls.

'If they haven't got one here, there's not one to be had,' he said.

He was right. There were trays of pearl rings and it took only a few minutes for Susan to home in on one. She compared its size with her mother's ring that she'd brought along.

'That's it,' she said. 'She'll love it. A huge pink pearl in a diamond cluster.'

'You've got a good eye, miss,' said the jeweller encouragingly.

Susan showed Peter the price. Twenty-two pounds ten, and he realised that the problem was up to him. He pointed out the yellowish diamond in the array of white stones, noted that the pearl was not perfectly spherical and mentioned that his father had the good Jewish name of Samuel. The price sank gently to the magical twenty.

Susan was almost skipping with delight as they walked on up to the top of Hatton Garden. As they turned right over the railway bridge the scene changed completely, with the prosperity of the jewellery area being replaced by the neglect of Clerkenwell. It had been an artisan clock-making area in the past, but was now slowly dying. Historic Clerkenwell Green was almost derelict. Finally Susan's curiosity got the better of her.

'So, where are we going?'

'To the council offices,' said Peter. 'They should be just down there.'

She blinked in surprise.

The offices were just what Peter expected—a huge Victorian edifice in dirty stone, almost next to an equally grubby tavern called "The Swan". Upstairs in a cramped oak panelled room was the planning department. It had two staff, an older woman with her hair in a bun and a young man. He looked approvingly at Susan's legs while his boss looked disgustedly at the length of her skirt.

Boss spoke first. Peter recognised her acid tones from yesterday's telephone call.

'You need help?'

'I'd like to look at all the planning applications approved over the last three months,' said Peter. 'And any pending.'

'They're here.' She retrieved three files from the shelf behind and put them on the desk. 'Bring them back when you've finished.'

Peter handed two files to Susan.

'Look for anything on change of use to animal facilities.' He saw the look on her face. 'I'll explain later.'

He quickly scanned through his file, found nothing and cautiously approached the Boss.

'I'm really not finding what I'm looking for,' he said. 'I just want to know if anyone's been enquiring about change of use to animal facilities.'

Leg Lover looked up excitedly. 'Well,' he said. 'There's—'

'There's nothing,' snapped Boss. 'We are only allowed to discuss plans actually in application.' She glared at Peter. 'If it's not in the file it's not happening.'

Peter retreated to the desk. He wrote a note on a piece of paper and tucked it into the file like a bookmark

'SEE YOU IN THE SWAN AT ONE'

'Take it over to him,' he said. 'And *smile*.'

Susan blinked at the note, then did as she was told. Leg Lover studied the message, looked up, and nodded with a grin. They returned their files and went down to the Swan. As they sat down Susan looked beseechingly at Peter.

'Okay, truth time,' he said. 'I'll get some drinks and tell you what's going on. What do you want?'

'A Babycham, please.'

In a corner he gave Susan a potted version of events.

'I heard through the grapevine that the Institute is planning a new animal house in Clerkenwell. I couldn't believe it. McDonald knows nothing about it. I got so curious I decided to find out what's going on.'

Susan was amazed. 'So why would they do it behind McDonald's back? It doesn't make sense.'

'I know,' he said. 'That's why we're here, playing spies. How do you feel about that, Miss Susan Mata Hari?'

She giggled.

'Look, there he is.' Peter nudged Susan. 'You talk to him nicely while I get him a drink.'

In true Mata Hari fashion Susan eased her skirt up over her knees.

Leg Lover was not best pleased to see Peter, but he accepted the offer of a pint of bitter. He sat hopefully next to Susan while Peter got the beer. Armed with his drink he started to whine.

'I'll lose my job if they find out I'm talking to you about work.'

'You're not,' said Peter. 'We met here by accident. So what do you know?' He slid two pound notes under the ashtray to encourage the flow of information.

Leg Lover tore his eyes from Susan's knees and fixated on the money.

'There's this factory,' he said. 'Just down the road from where I live. Been empty for years. Then recently there's been a lot of activity there, and it's been sold. About three weeks ago a man asked about using it for animals. But he never came back.'

'What did he look like?'

'Don't really remember. Small man, neatly dressed.'

'That's not much for two pounds,' snapped Peter.

Leg Lover grabbed the money. 'That's all I know, tough if it's not enough.'

'So where is it?' asked Peter, and Leg Lover wrote down the address.

'Go down the road here, it's the fourth street on the right, about a hundred yards up.'

The factory looked rather like a large Wesleyan chapel, set in a sea of cracked concrete. There was a double door at one end and a van parked outside, and from inside they could hear hammering. Peter eased the door open and they went into what looked like a small engineering facility, with steel hoists suspended from the roof. The two men who were busy chiselling into the brickwork stopped when they saw their visitors and moved silently forward, approaching Peter and Susan from both sides in a pincer movement. Their menace was palpable. Peter remembered his military training. *Distraction.* He picked up a cold chisel and slapped it onto his hand. The men stopped.

'What do you want?' said the swarthy one.

'We came to see the factory,' said Peter. 'We heard it was for sale.'

The men advanced again.

'Who sent you?'

'Johnsons.' Peter remembered the name on a board lying on the ground outside. The men were almost upon them.

'I don't believe you. Johnson's dealt with the sale weeks ago. You're a bloody liar, and a snoop.'

'Out,' snapped the second man. He shoved Susan on her shoulder. Peter turned to protect her, and with an expert move, the first man grabbed the chisel and rammed Peter's arm up behind his back. His shoulder cracked. Next Peter felt a foot in his back, and he was hurled through the door. After him came Susan, catching her heel on the step. The door slammed behind her, smashing off the heel and ramming into her foot. She screamed and fell down. Behind them they heard the door bolts ram home.

'They were my best shoes,' she sobbed.

Peter bent down and looked at her foot. It was bruised and already he could see the swelling.

'Dear God, Susan, I'm so sorry. I didn't expect this.' He was grey with pain and guilt. He took off her good shoe. 'Can you walk?'

'I think so. I'll try.'

He locked his good arm under hers and lifted her up. She wobbled and he put his arm around her to steady her. Together they hobbled painfully down to the main road where Peter frantically hailed a taxi. It stopped and the driver looked sympathetically at the shoeless Susan.

'In trouble?'

'She broke her heel and hurt her foot,' said Peter. 'Lincoln's Inn Fields, please.'

'Yes guv.'

In the cab Susan sat slumped in the corner.

'What's going on, Peter?' she whispered. 'What's all this about?'

'I don't know, Susan, I really don't.' He saw that the swelling was worse. He tapped on the partition window.

'Driver, I've changed my mind. Liverpool Street station, please.'

He sat back next to Susan, marshalled his thoughts and told her everything, summing it all up at the end.

'So there it is, Susan. Team losing contracts without good reason, Lomax humiliating him publicly, Lomax with some sort of hold over Team, Lomax wanting testing and getting secret animal facilities. I was curious, I thought it could be all coincidence, but not after today.'

Susan sat thinking. 'Those men weren't proper electricians,' she said suddenly. 'No one puts in electrical sockets at overhead height.'

'Were they doing that?' asked Peter incredulously.

'Oh yes,' she said. 'Dad was an electrician, so I noticed what they were doing.'

They nursed their pain in a silence which lasted till Liverpool Street, where Peter bought a return ticket to Ilford.

'You don't need to see me home,' protested Susan. 'I'll be fine. I'll take a taxi from the station.'

'Right,' he said. 'But I'll make sure you get in it. That's the least I can do after all this.'

'Fine. Thank you, Peter.'

The train compartment was empty and Susan sat down gratefully, keeping her foot off the ground. She automatically checked that she had her purse, felt the rings inside it, and remembered her mother. Peter examined her foot again.

'I think the swelling's stopped,' he said. 'But you must call me tonight and tell me.'

'Won't Anne mind?'

'It doesn't matter if she does.'

Despite the pain, Susan felt strangely happy. She enjoyed having Peter fuss over her, she enjoyed sharing secrets and she liked having him as a friend, but she knew she had to give more if she wanted him as a confidante.

'Peter,' she said. 'You remember you asked about Mum yesterday. If you want, I'll tell you now.'

She was near exhaustion, and so the story came out in dribs and drabs, but Peter finally pieced it all together. Susan's electrician father had been killed in an accident at Dagenham, and her mother, who had been a veterinary nurse, had used the insurance money to set up a pet shop with a partner. At first they had done well, but the partner had gradually become less trustworthy and had finally absconded with most of their funds. Her mother was forced to sell the shop to pay off some of the debt and to re-mortgage their house to finance the rest. With the shop gone, her mother had no income at all.

'Dear God,' said Peter. 'Why on earth didn't you tell me all this before?'

'It's Mum. It's her pride. She didn't want anyone to know and she swore me to secrecy. She feels she's lost Dad and squandered his money. What she really needs is a well-paid job and that's not easy at forty-eight.'

'That's a tough one,' he said. 'But your story's safe with me. I won't tell anyone, not even Anne. And Susan.' He hesitated. 'Today's events need to be just between us two.'

She nodded.

At Ilford he put her into a taxi.

'Give it a long soak in iced water,' he said. 'And do call me. I need to know how you're doing.'

'Yes Peter. And thanks.'

'Don't thank me,' he retorted. 'You should be cursing me for all I've put you through.'

Back on the train, ready to cross London to Paddington, Peter realised how much his arm was hurting. His worry about Susan had suppressed it till then. He gingerly took off his coat and jacket and tucked his right hand inside his shirt. He buttoned up the shirt and with that support the pain subsided and stayed bearable for the rest of the journey.

At Paddington he called Anne.

'Peter, where are you?'

'Paddington, on the way home. Anne, I need—'

'I called you this morning,' she interrupted reprovingly. 'Where on earth were you?'

'Hatton Garden, buying jewellery.'

'So who's the lucky lady?'

'She'll know at Christmas,' said Peter, thinking quickly.

Anne smiled. Peter had good taste in jewellery.

Peter persisted. 'Anne, listen. I've—I've—I'm feeling awful. Can you meet me? Twenty five past. Sorry, got to go.'

The train was packed, so Peter took a first-class seat and hoped the ticket inspector wouldn't catch him. All went well until he started up the stairs at Maidenhead, obediently following the instructions to 'keep to the right'. Fatigue made him stumble, and he instinctively wrenched his right arm out of his jacket to grab the rail. There was a loud crack, and the pain seared down his arm. The last thing he saw before he fainted was Anne running frantically down the steps towards him.

Chapter 4
Cambridge

The houseman at Reading Hospital was pleasant but assertive.

'I'm sorry Mrs Stott, but your husband shouldn't go home tonight. We need to keep him in for observation—certainly until tomorrow.'

'But he seems so bright and bouncy,' protested Anne.

'That's the morphine talking. He was unconscious most of the way here in the ambulance, and then he was sick. So he may have delayed concussion. His X-rays show that he didn't fracture his skull or his arm, though that's one hell of a dislocation. We'll have to ring you in the morning after the rounds and tell you if he's okay. You should be able to collect him then.'

'Right,' she said. 'Thank you, doctor. I'd better tell him the bad news.'

Peter was sitting up in bed, loudly explaining his theories on cancer to an admiring nurse. His face fell when he heard the news. He tried to argue, but Anne pushed him firmly back onto the pillows.

'You just stay there,' she said sternly. 'And stop boring the staff.'

'Yes, boss.'

She kissed him and stepped back. 'It's funny,' she said. 'With all this worry I don't feel hungry. I don't want to eat and I don't feel sick either. Bye darling. See you tomorrow.'

She drove home carefully and parked the MG in the garage. As she opened the front door the telephone was ringing.

'Hello, Mrs Stott,' said Susan. 'I'm ringing P—Dr Stott to say I won't be in tomorrow.'

Anne was curious. Susan had never rung in the evening before.

'I'll tell him tomorrow. I'm sure he won't be back at work for days. He's in hospital.'

'Hospital.' Susan almost screamed down the phone 'Dear God, how bad is it?'

'He's dislocated his arm, and he's got a slightly cut head and concussion. But they say he should be home by tomorrow.' Anne started to explain, but all she could hear was Susan saying, 'I'm so sorry.' The phone clicked.

Anne sat still, trying to get her thoughts in order and to make sense of the day. Finally, exhaustion took over and she fell into bed. Normally she didn't sleep well when she was stressed, but this time she stayed out cold until eight. She reached out to Peter for comfort, but he wasn't there and she felt guilty that she hadn't thought about him all night. Instantly she rang the hospital, where the sister said that he'd had a good night. Encouraged, she made some porridge with milk and took it up to bed, and to her delight it stayed down. She knew the hospital wouldn't phone until after ward rounds and so she let herself to drift off to sleep till midmorning. When she finally woke she phoned Lomax's secretary to say that Peter was in hospital, and then asked the telephonist to put her through to the lab.

'This is Oncology,' said a familiar voice. 'Can I help you?'

'I thought you weren't going in today, Susan?'

'You're right, Mrs Stott, I wasn't. But I thought I'd better see that things are still progressing.'

'That's very good of you,' said Anne sarcastically. 'Considering you were so upset last night.'

'You're right, I was upset. Dr Stott's big conference is coming up next week and he'll miss it. It's a really important paper in front of the real world experts.'

'I don't think the injury has stopped his brain or voice working,' snapped Anne. 'He'll be there.'

'Good,' said Susan 'Thank you Mrs Stott. And how is he?'

Anne put the receiver down.

She was cautiously eating a piece of dry toast when the phone rang again and she recognised Lomax's clipped BBC accent.

'Hello, Mrs Stott. I've just heard the bad news. Is Peter alright?'

Anne explained about the injury.

'So how did it happen?'

'He tripped at the station.'

'Really?' The Director sounded incredulous. 'It seems a bad injury from such a small thing.'

'Yes, I'm surprised how bad it is,' said Anne. 'But I was there, I saw it happen.'

'Really?' This time Lomax seemed confused. 'You did? Well, he seems—very unlucky. Please give him my regards. We need him back soon.'

Anne killed time for the rest of the morning. She was becoming increasingly queasy and knew that she wouldn't be able to drive if the sickness got worse. Finally she went upstairs and made herself sick, and she was washing her face when the phone rang again. It was that nice houseman from the hospital.

'He's all yours, Mrs Stott. Cross, but all yours. You can collect him any time you want.'

Anne put on her fur coat and gloves. She needed air on her face to stop feeling sick, so she took down the top of the MG. At the traffic lights on the edge of town a lorry drew up alongside, and she could feel the driver looking down at her. She knew exactly what he was looking at: a slim, attractive brunette in a white convertible—the ultimate in desirability. Then the lights changed, the lorry driver returned to his gears, and the smiling Anne sped off to collect her husband.

Anne expected that Peter would make a bad patient, and she was right. He was normally very fit, and now hated being ill and not being able to use his right hand. Eventually she settled him on the sofa with the radio and telephone on his left. He dozed most of the day while Anne cautiously drank small amounts of milk shake. Exhausted, they went to bed early.

The letter was on the mat when Anne went down next morning. She took some tea up to Peter and made sure he'd taken his pain pills.

'Mum's definitely coming,' she said. 'And obviously looking forward to it. I'd completely forgotten about her with all this. I need to do some shopping.'

'She doesn't realise she's coming to a disaster area,' snarled Peter.

After breakfast and some good coffee he felt better and rang the department, and was amazed to hear that Susan was at work.

'I rang you yesterday,' she said. 'Didn't Anne tell you? What are we going to do about the conference?'

'You were in yesterday? Dear God, you didn't need to do *that*. How on earth did you manage it?'

'Mum cut up one of her slippers. She took the heel off and bandaged the whole thing onto my foot. It wasn't too bad—I went in late and everyone gave up their seat for me. And I used a taxi. I look like Mrs Mop. But how are you?'

Peter explained about his arm. 'But I'm damned if I'll miss the conference. I'll just miss the first day, Tuesday, and go on Wednesday and give the talk. So I'll come in on Monday, come Anne, hell and high water, and run through it with you. So expect me then, but I'll be late.'

The conversation then turned to progress in the department and how the cell culture was going, with both speakers avoiding the subject foremost in their minds. Then Susan finally bit the bullet.

'What about us, Peter? The factory, those men? What should we do?'

'I don't know, Susan. I really don't. I've thought and thought about it. Should we have called the police? Should I tell Anne? I just don't know. Let's leave it till Monday.'

'Right, Peter,' she said. She had never known him so unsure and undecided. 'We'll do that. Leave it till then. And Peter.' She hesitated. 'Look after yourself.'

During the next two days, Peter's temper and health improved. The pain subsided and he got used to moving around with a sling on his arm. Meanwhile, Anne worked determinedly on the house, getting it into the state of perfect cleanliness that she deemed essential for her visiting mother.

'She's your mum,' complained Peter. 'Not the Queen. Her cottage isn't *this* clean.'

'I know. But I was such a slob when I lived at home. This is to show that I'm a reformed woman, coping perfectly well with house, husband, and pregnancy.'

Peter laughed. 'Then I'll have to reform too.'

On Saturday everything went to plan. Mum's phone call came at seven and they got to the station on good time, and as the compartment door swung open an older version of Anne stepped onto the platform. The similarity was so exact, they could have been sisters. Anne's mother had kept her figure, her face was virtually unlined, and Peter, when he decided to marry Anne, had known exactly what he was getting. He watched as the two women hugged each other and saw the tears in their eyes Then Mum turned to him. She moved to hug him, then jumped back.

'Peter, what have you done?' Her voice had the soft lilt of the Hebrides. 'What's happened to my favourite son-in-law?'

Peter grinned. 'He's only dislocated his shoulder. But he's very pleased to see his favourite mother-in-law.' He kissed her on the cheek, and they walked to the taxi while a porter manhandled her suitcase. In the cab she examined her family.

'I've seen you both looking better,' she observed. 'You're both pale as ghosts.'

'She's had morning sickness,' said Peter. 'With me, it's the arm, it's still hurting. I should have taken more pills.'

'Right,' said Mum. 'But I'm here now. Just sit back, relax, and let me look after you both for a week and a day.'

Peter and Anne exchanged glances. 'Thank you, Mum,' said Anne. 'That would be marvellous.'

Anne was nothing if not enthusiastic. At home she cheerfully rushed in to make coffee for her mother, smelt the aroma of the roasted beans and rushed upstairs to be sick. From the sitting room they could hear her retching into the toilet.

'That's how it is,' said Peter. 'It's been like this all along.'

'I thought it might be bad,' said his mother-in-law. 'But nothing like this.'

'What made you think that?'

Mum looked embarrassed. 'History, I suppose. My sister had it badly and so did I. So I thought Anne might get it too.'

'Oh,' said Peter. He didn't know morning sickness ran in families, and made a mental note to look it up.

Over the weekend Peter and Anne realised what a god-send Mum was. She watched Anne like a hawk, made sure she took regular small amounts of milk shake, and waited hand and foot on Peter. Not having to help Anne meant he didn't have to move very much and the pain improved. Mum insisted on going to church on Sunday. A devout Presbyterian, she hadn't missed a weekend service for years. Anne had given up on religion years ago, but she went along to keep her mother company and to prevent any ill-feeling. Peter took a short walk and found that he could manage quite easily as long as his shoulder was firmly strapped.

Next morning Anne drove Peter to the station and insisted that he travel first class.

'You can't risk bumping it,' she said. 'I know it's expensive, but we can afford it. Now look after yourself, and watch those steps.'

'You're becoming a real nag,' he replied. 'But I'll be damned careful. I'll ring you. Hope you two will be all right.'

'It's been okay so far,' she replied. 'Mum's been fine.'

Peter had hoped to spend all of the morning practising his talk, but it was not to be. Instead, he got a pleasant surprise. It was the conference organiser on the phone:

'Peter, I have a favour to ask. Could you chair Wednesday's meeting? Johnson, who was going to do it, is ill. You'll need to give an overview of all the talks at the end, plus a summary of progress so far. And you could chip in with an update on your He-La project.'

Peter was totally amazed at the unexpected honour, and could only splutter out a delighted 'Yes'. His next need was to get fully updated on progress in the department, and he walked down the corridor to room 306, known to the staff as the "Heels Room". Heels was a departmental "in word", a contraction of the correct title of He-La, which in turn was an abbreviation of the name of the original donor of the cells. She was a certain Henrietta Lacks, who had died of cervical cancer in 1951. A sample of her tumour cells had been taken before her death and placed in a nutrient medium where they continued to grow. They were still growing in 1963.

The Heels room was hot. It needed to be to keep the cells alive. Some had been flown in from the States a year ago, and were now growing in flat bottles containing the pink growth medium. A rack of the bottles rocked slowly, keeping the nutrient mixed and sending waves of pink liquid surging against the glass. As the cells multiplied the liquid turned milky, and it reminded Peter of a diluted version of Anne's pregnancy diet. Anne would never be immortal, though she might be immortalised as a great painter, but Henrietta Lacks had achieved immortality. Her He-La cells would be dividing relentlessly long after she was dust in a Baltimore graveyard.

The cells were a marvellous tool for testing out anti-cancer drugs. The holy grail of cancer research was a process which killed off all cancer cells, but that was unrealistic. A lot of chemicals killed cancer cells, but they killed healthy cells too. A drug which slowed the growth of cancer cells without any collateral damage was a more realistic option, and using the Heels was a quick and convenient method of finding out which drug had anti-cancer properties. The final tests on animals, which were required by law, would evaluate the drug's overall toxicity.

In the room a technician was carefully inoculating fresh pink bottles with live He-La cells. Peter watched carefully as he heated a loop of platinum wire to red heat and then plunged it into the jar of live cells. The drop of liquid containing the cells was then transferred to the test bottle. The boy knew his job. Peter waited for him to finish before speaking.

'How's it going?'

The technician blushed at being spoken to by his boss.

'It seems fine, Dr Stott. I've just given the latest results to Susan. The fluorouracil seems to slow the growth, even at really low levels.'

'How low?'

'I think about 0.1 milligrams per litre.'

'Wow!' said Peter. 'Excellent. Keep up the good work.'

The boy blushed again. 'I'll try. Thank you, Dr Stott.'

As Peter returned to the office Susan arrived from her coffee break. He grinned at her slippered foot.

'Nice to see you,' he said. 'But you're right. You do look like Mrs Mop. How is it?'

'It's getting better, slowly. But it's so swollen I still have to use the slipper. But how about you? You look really pale.'

'I'm fine if I don't move it,' said Peter. 'But forget that, it's the talk we've got to go through. And I'll need an update on the Heels.'

'It's all set up. I'll get you a coffee and we can start then if you want.'

In the lecture theatre, they went through the talk slide by slide, but it was too long. Then Peter adjusted his delivery and the whole thing gelled. On the third run it was perfect, and so they did it a fourth time to make sure everything went smoothly, and on that moment of triumph they went off to eat. Susan volunteered to get their lunches, and while Peter was searching for a table he saw Ron Team sitting in a corner. The Head of Pharmacology waved weakly at him.

'Glad to see you, Peter. How's the arm?'

'It's getting better, but how are you, Ron? You look awful.'

Team sat back, smiling wryly.

'That obvious, is it? They say it never rains but it pours, and it's been pouring for days. So what do you want to hear first? The worst or the least worst?'

'I think the least worst,' said Peter cautiously.

'Peter, you know when we last talked you said I should find out about all the other viromycin contracts. And, after dithering, I did. And do you know, Peter.' He hesitated, putting edge into his words. 'All their contracts are going ahead. Only *mine* were cancelled.'

Jesus, thought Peter. *They don't get much worse than that.*

'Then there's the worst,' Team continued remorselessly. 'It's Janet—my wife. She's got—she's got to have an operation. It's serious. But Paul Stephens says he'll help out and do the surgery at the Marsden.'

Peter knew Stephens' speciality, so he didn't need to enquire about the nature of Janet's disease.

'Dear God,' he said. 'Poor Janet. That really is cruel. But Paul's a real professional.'

'Yes, he is,' said Team, cheering up slightly. 'Look, there he is now.'

In the distance, Peter could see the Head of Surgery approaching.

'I'll leave you to it,' he said. 'I'm sure you've got lots to talk about.'

'Yes, we do. Thanks, Peter. By the way, good luck on Wednesday. Give my love to Mark's, my old alma mater. They do a good lunch.'

Peter gripped Team's shoulder. 'Thanks, Ron, keep your chin up.'

He joined Susan at their table. As they ate she updated him on progress with the cells.

'That's it,' she said. 'Oh, I nearly forgot, I have to thank you. Mum loves her ring.'

'Good,' said Peter. 'It's nice she's had a treat.' He hesitated. 'Susan, I think I will need your help on Wednesday. In the overall summary I'll need to jiggle all the slides and so I need someone who I trust to do that. And you could see how they react to your He-La results.'

'Could I come?' she was amazed. 'I'm not a member.'

'You'd be my guest,' said her boss. 'We're allowed guests. I used to go with my Prof when I was a student. So do come. I'm sure you'll find it interesting.'

Susan's face shone. 'I'd love to.'

'Right. I'll ring and book an extra lunch.'

As the day progressed Peter's arm got steadily worse and he decided to call it a day.

'I may not be in tomorrow,' he told Susan. 'I'll see how the arm is. If not, I'll see you under the clock at King's Cross at ten to eight on Wednesday.'

Susan beamed. 'I'll be there. Early. And I'm really looking forward to it. Thanks for asking me, Peter.'

'It's nothing,' he protested. 'No more than you deserve. We make a good team.'

At home, Anne had had a reasonably good day, with only mild sickness, but during the evening and night it got worse, and by Tuesday morning she was too exhausted to move.

'I don't like this at all,' said Mum. 'Peter, she needs a doctor.'

He nodded. 'I'll ring him. You're right. We've put this off too long.'

Dr James was very concerned as he watched Anne retch continuously into an almost empty bowl.

'I'll give her an injection to stop this,' he said. 'But we'll have to find something she can keep down or she may end up in hospital. You say she was reasonably alright on milk and milk shake?'

'Yes, till now'

'It could be the fat. Try her with skimmed milk with a bit of flavouring. I'll ring this afternoon to see what's happening.'

'Thank you,' said Peter. 'Thank you, doctor. I do appreciate this.'

Mum put on slacks and rode Peter's bike into town to get the skimmed milk. Anne drank it tentatively and it stayed down. They increased her intake slowly through the day and it still stayed down. Dr James was impressed when he rang back.

'Sounds good,' he said. 'If she's the same overnight we may have cracked it. You must call me if she isn't.'

Peter was so worried that he actively considered not going to Cambridge, but Mum would have none of it.

'You've got to go,' she said. 'It's your big day. I'll look after her for you.'

'Right.' Peter was convinced at last. 'But I'll call you when I get there to see how things are. And thanks, Mum.'

''No need, Peter. What are Mums for?'

Their train arrived on time in Cambridge and Peter called Mum from the kiosk in the foyer. She said that Anne was sleeping peacefully and had not been sick.

'Stop worrying,' she said. 'Impress them.'

In the forecourt Peter and Susan got into a taxi.

'Where to, sir?'

'Addenbrookes, please'

'Which one, sir?'

Peter remembered that the hospital was expanding to a new site.

'The old one,' he said, 'Trumpington Road.'

It really was Peter's day. He opened the meeting, introduced the speakers and charmed everyone. His lecture was the last one of the morning, and Susan was at the back of the theatre operating the projector while he was on stage talking about the slides. He was on slide two when it happened. The door at the back opened suddenly and a man looked in, his face reflected in the light from the corridor. Susan jumped back in horror, pressed the wrong button, and slide five appeared on the screen. Peter looked confused, and the audience stirred in embarrassment.

'Wrong slide, Susan, we're on number two. Back three, please.'

Susan's concentration returned. She found the correct slide, and then looked nervously at the door. The man had gone. After that the lecture went really well, and at the end Peter summed all the speakers' work, answered questions and received admiring applause. Finally, as the delegates drifted off to lunch, he went to find Susan. He expected congratulations, but found her tense and almost in tears.

'It's all right, Susan,' he said sympathetically. 'It was only a little setback, the slide. Didn't affect anything. They liked it.'

'It's not that.' Her face was pale. 'It was *him*. He came in at the back. I saw him and jumped, and pressed the forward button.'

'Him?'

'The man at the factory. The one who did in your arm.'

'Dear God, it can't be. Are you sure?'

'That's it,' she said. 'I can't be sure. It was only a glimpse, but it looked like him.' She shuddered. 'Those eyes. He really scared me.'

'It couldn't have been him,' said Peter firmly. 'You must have been mistaken. What would he be doing here?'

That question, and its possible answers, would resonate in his head for days.

'You're right,' replied Susan, partially convinced. 'It must have been someone else.'

By that time the theatre had almost emptied and one of the last delegates approached them cautiously.

'You're going to lunch?' he asked. 'I've been asked to be a sweeper—make sure everyone gets to Mark's on time. It's only a short walk.' Then he noticed Susan's foot. 'Oh.'

'We'll need a taxi,' said Peter.

Outside they eventually found a taxi driver who didn't mind going the short distance to Mark's. Inside the cab Susan momentarily forgot the incident in the theatre and eyed up their rather handsome guide.

'You've been to Mark's before?' she asked.

'Oh yes,' he grinned. 'Practically live there. I'm a Fellow.'

Susan wasn't quite sure what a Fellow was. Some sort of tutor? At Barking Tech teachers taught their subject and were called lecturers.

'So, what does a Fellow do?'

'I do some teaching, and give tutorials on a one-to-one basis. That means I get to know the students really well and I can keep them on track. If they fall behind I have to crack the whip a bit.' He grinned again. 'My tutor did that to me. I spent the first two years at Mark's at parties and playing tennis. Then he read the riot act to me. I started to work and got a First. Then I did my doctorate with *Crick.*' He stressed the name Crick for the benefit of his audience, making sure they knew he had worked with the most famous biochemist of the decade. 'Then I stayed on as a Fellow. A sort of poacher turned gamekeeper.'

Susan was already getting tired of him. She hated show-offs. 'You'll enjoy the lunch,' continued the Fellow. 'I've seen the menu. 'They're doing us proud today.'

Susan's jaw dropped when she saw the medieval dining hall with its vaulted room and oak beams. They sat at ancient trencher tables and ate excellent food washed down with fine wine. The overall mix of riches, power, history and privilege was palpable. The Fellow stayed with them, hopefully chatting up Susan and offering to show them around after lunch.

'You've got to see the science bridge,' he said. 'And the library.'

So they did the tour, crossing the bridge over the Cam which joined the two halves of the college, and then on to the library.

'It's all here,' said the Fellow. 'Everything that's happened over the past four hundred years. Even *me.*' He produced a photographic album and displayed a snap of himself in his tennis shorts.

'Singles tennis champion in 1956,' he said proudly. Susan and Peter made their congratulatory noises, and then the two men wandered off to look at the scientific books while Susan continued flipping through the album. She liked fashion, and giggled at the length of the shorts and skirts as the photos aged. Suddenly she went silent. She looked up, caught Peter's eye, and waved him over.

The photo was of two men. A young ascetic Sherlock Holmes stood next to his strikingly handsome blond playing partner. The inscription below said it all.

> *The men's doubles champions for 1923*
> *Mr John Lomax and Mr Ronald Team*

Peter just sat there, staring, taking it all in.
'Bastards,' he muttered under his breath. 'Double bastards.'
'You know them?' asked the Fellow, seeing the interest.
'Yes,' said Peter bitterly. 'They're my *colleagues.*'

He continued staring at the photo, and then finally remembered his manners.

'Thanks so much for all your help,' he said to the Fellow. 'We really do appreciate it. But I think it's time to go. Do you think you could get us a taxi?'

Neither Peter nor Susan spoke in the cab, and they spoke only a little on the train. Susan's thoughts alternatively swung between the man who had frightened her and the tennis photo, while Peter's concentrated on Team. 'We'll discuss it all in detail tomorrow,' he said, 'every bit of it. After I've talked to Ron. He's a friend.'

'You're sure?' Susan was being unusually assertive. 'You said we'd talk on Monday, but we didn't.'

'Tomorrow. On my honour, Susan. After Ron.'

She nodded in approval.

At home Mum and Anne were delighted to see Peter. Anne had had a good day and Dr James had looked in to see if things were going well. If the sickness started again, he had another remedy in reserve. Mum cooked Peter some congratulatory lamb chops while Anne munched carefully on Weetabix with skimmed milk. Both were hugely pleased at his success, and Anne opened a bottle of claret that Peter's Dad had laid down before he died. She even had a cautious sip with no ill effects.

'Surely don't need to go to work tomorrow,' she pleaded. 'You look shattered.'

'Sorry, darling, it's a must. I've promised. But I guarantee I'll take Friday off. Maybe we could take Mum to Henley and Wallingford, see the sights.'

She had to make do with that.

Peter made a huge effort to get to work early, but Susan was there before him. She looked hard at him as he arrived.

'Yes,' he said. 'As promised. I'll see Ron first.'

He rang Team's secretary who said she'd call him when Ron got in. He noticed how tired Susan looked.

'Susan,' he said. 'I'm shattered. You look exhausted— you've worked so hard through all this. I'm having a day off tomorrow—why don't you do the same?'

She smiled. 'That would be nice. I'd like a long weekend.'

The phone rang and Peter went downstairs to see Team, who was sitting relaxed in his chair with his feet on the table.

'How are you, Ron? How are things with you and Janet?'

Team smiled. 'Going well, I hope, Peter. They took Janet in on Tuesday and Paul did the op on Wednesday—yesterday. She was fine last night and Paul's very hopeful about everything. So I'm as happy as I can be. I'm off to see her after lunch.'

'I'm so glad,' said Peter. 'You two deserve a bit of luck.'

'And what's your news, Peter? How was Mark's?'

'The food was superb,' said Peter. 'Like you said. I'm surprised you and John Lomax didn't put on weight after three years of that.'

'Well, I did put on some weight,' replied Team. 'But I can't answer for John. He was two years ahead of me and we hardly knew each other while we were there. It's a big college and final years didn't mix with humble firsts.'

The first lie, thought Peter. *And there will be more.* There were. Team kept on embroidering his fabrications with statements like 'we didn't mix in the same social circles' and 'our tastes were very different', until Peter had had enough. He decided to end the conversation with a question.

'So you enjoyed Mark's?'

The answer was curiously enigmatic.

'It made me what I am.'

Peter left Team's office and walked slowly upstairs to his own room, shutting the door firmly. His staff knew that look. *Do not disturb*. He sat down at his desk, thinking, his cold rage pushing his brain into overdrive. Having his arm dislocated had scared him, made him indecisive, but Team's lies had put steel into his backbone. He knew he was committed. The overriding characteristic of all scientists is curiosity, and Peter knew he could never live with himself until he knew exactly what was going on. He outlined a plan of action on a notepad, and then went to the door.

'Susan,' he called. 'We need to have that talk.'

The staff in the lab glanced at each other. Those words usually meant trouble for the recipient.

Chapter 5
Mata Hari

Next morning Susan sat excitedly on the train as it clickedy-clicked its way over the Fens to Cambridge. She had been going to take a day's holiday, a day for relaxation, but this was even better. Peter had trusted her with the investigation, and she was determined not to let him down.

'The answer has to be in Cambridge,' he'd said. 'The fact that Lomax and Team were at the same college is no secret. It's in their CVs. It's that Team tried to keep their close association secret that really intrigues me. They were only at the college together for one academic year, and that really means only from October to May, when Lomax left Cambridge to start his Ph.D. at Imperial. So what they want concealed must have occurred during those eight months. That narrows the field down. So I want you to go down there, and start digging. Try the local rag, and look for anything unusual that happened at Mark's in those eight months. Also look at the records, who the Master was, the Fellows, the sporting clique. Any famous alumni. Anything. We may be clutching at straws, but we've got to start somewhere.'

'Maybe I should ring that awful Fellow,' said Susan doubtfully. 'He could get me clearance for the library and help out.'

'A good idea,' agreed Peter. 'Ring him. And Susan, keep this quiet. Just tell me how much it costs you and I'll give you the cash. Put nothing through accounts.'

'Yes, Peter.'

'Our other prong is the two companies; Ciencia, who holds the patent, and Thirsk. You'll need to go to the Patent Office and Companies House. Find out who the directors are, where the money is. All of that. I'll just tell everyone you're doing research on my behalf—which is actually the truth. You're going to have to be a proper little Mata Hari.'

'I thought the real Mata Hari was quite improper,' giggled Susan.

'You don't need to go *that* far. And Susan, are you sure you want this? Say no now and we'll drop it like a brick.'

'I'm up for it Peter. You know that. As you said, we make a good team. I really can't wait to get going.'

Susan started the legwork that very afternoon without telling Peter. She rang the Fellow, who was delighted to hear from her and arranged a visit to the library in return for a promise of lunch tomorrow. She found out the name of the local newspaper and arranged to see the back copies for 1923 and 1924. With that done, she mentally decided on an outfit bad enough to repel her academic admirer and went home in a state of excited expectation.

When Susan got to Mark's, the porter said he was expecting her. He took her to the library and handed her a note.

'Sorry, lecturing this morning. I'll pick you up for lunch at 1:15. Love, John.'

Ugh, she thought.

She worked hard through the records for the next two hours, and learned only two interesting facts. The Master of the college in 1923 had been Professor Robert Napier, a pathologist from Addenbrookes, and that the men's singles tennis champion for that year had been a certain John Napier. She made a note to look into that odd coincidence. It was an unusual name.

Then the Fellow arrived.

'Lovely to see you,' he gushed, and Susan let him kiss her on the cheek. 'I booked a table at James's. It's where Crick and I used to go.'

Dear God, thought Susan, *does he never let up?*

'I'm looking forward to seeing it,' she replied untruthfully, realising that being a Mata Hari was not going to be all fun and games.

In the restaurant Susan quietly asked the manager to book a taxi for 2:30. Then she sat down with John and made an effort to be pleasant, and the lunch actually went rather well. Susan soon realised that the Fellow had an encyclopaedic knowledge of

Mark's and that when he wasn't boasting he was quite amusing company. He was also useful.

'I see that one of your past Masters was a Professor Napier,' she said. 'A pathologist. Isn't that unusual?'

The Fellow scratched his head.

'Not really. Anyone with a brilliant record can become Master. He got in a lot of money for Mark's and Addenbrookes. Actually he stayed on as Master till after the war, and he only died six months ago at some enormous age. Bright as a button right to the end, they say. They held a requiem for him two weeks ago.'

'Was he married?'

The Fellow grinned. 'Seems he wasn't that way inclined. Apparently when he was young he swung both ways, then ended up on one side.'

Susan's knowledge of homosexuality was vague.

'Ended up on one side?'

'He liked men.'

'So he didn't have any children,' persisted Susan.

'None that he would admit to. No, none. He left all his money to the College.'

The enquiry into life at Mark's got Susan through the soup and meat courses, and after a good desert and coffee she looked at her watch.

'Sorry John, I've got to go. Thanks for such a nice lunch.' She gave him a peck on the cheek. 'There's my taxi.'

'So where are you off to?' he asked.

'The station, then home,' lied Susan.

'Will I see you again?'

'I'll call you,' she said, lying again. 'Bye John. Thanks for everything.'

The taxi actually took her to the Gazette office where Susan checked the closing time, five o'clock, and asked the driver to collect her then. Inside she met the receptionist, a charming girl who had gone out of her way to be helpful.

'Hello, Miss Preston. I've got the folios for 1923 and 1924 for you. Call me if you need any help.'

Susan thanked her and sat down at the table. She started with the edition for the first week in October 1923. The Gazette was a weekly paper and so she had about 36 more additions to check through before she got to the following May. She forced herself to be systematic, to look at all the news pages and, at the umpteenth attempt, she found something. It was a double column entry from Friday the 15th of May 1924, and as she read it and re-read it her heart pounded and her face flushed in triumph. *Bingo*. The first chink of light.

Body of a Student Found

The body of Miss Laura Marshall, a student of Mark's college, was discovered floating in the River Cam on Monday. Her body was formally identified by her parents yesterday. Miss Marshall was engaged to Mr John Napier, also a student of Mark's college, who is believed to be at a tennis tournament in Paris.

The article didn't tell the whole story; surely there *must* have been an inquest. Susan looked frantically through the later editions. Nothing. She knew she was racing against the five o'clock closure, and when she saw the taxi arrive she realised she'd lost.

'Thanks so much for your help,' she said as she walked by the reception desk. 'I'm not finished yet. I'll have to come back next week.'

The receptionist smiled. 'Fine, I'm sure we'll still be here.'

On the train home Susan felt truly proud at the progress on her first day. She would call Peter when she got home and tell him her news.

Her boss and his family had also had a good day. Anne had woken free of sickness with a trace of colour in her cheeks, and after a late breakfast they set off for Henley. Anne drove, and Mum and Peter took turns sitting in the small back seat. He had taken a double dose of pills to make sure he was free of pain, and Anne had a supply of skimmed milk and Weetabix. It was a clear, cracklingly cold day after an early frost, and Henley looked stunning in the autumn sun. There were a few rowers on the river.

'Jack would have loved it here,' said Mum to Peter. 'He used to row at school, and Henley's the Mecca for it. It's such a pity he's not here to see it.'

Anne drove on, tight-lipped.

In Nettlebed, in the middle of the Chilterns they stopped, and Anne topped up on her staple diet while Mum and Peter swapped seats. Then they drove on into Wallingford, where Anne went shopping while the other two ate lunch. From the restaurant window they could see her as she pottered about in the Market Square, excitedly looking for baby things.

'It's lovely to see her so happy,' said Mum.

'Yes,' said her son-in-law. 'Anne's the best thing that's happened to me.'

'I can see that. You're good for her, Peter. Her dad would have loved to have seen her like this. She was the most important thing in Jack's life.'

Anne hardly ever talked about her father, so Peter probed further.

'It must have been awful, him dying so young. Of a heart attack of all things. At his age.'

Mum took her time answering. 'His death certificate said a heart attack. But he really died of despair. When you stop believing in what you stand for you've nothing to live for. And a minister has to have belief. *I still do.*'

The stress on the last three words warned Peter to be cautious.

'I can see that,' he said. 'Religion is obviously a great comfort to you.'

She smiled. 'Yes, it is. Sorry, Peter. You hit a nerve. But it was such a waste of a good man.'

'No apology needed, Mum. Come on, eat up, it's getting cold. And Mum—thanks for everything. Helping out like this.'

By the time they got to the pudding the shops had closed for lunch and Anne arrived with her purchases—patterns, wool, and knitting needles. They had tea instead of coffee, and Anne drank her first cup in days with no ill effect.

Peter wanted to show Mum another of his favourite spots, so they drove out of Wallingford and up a track onto the Downs. The scene was breathtaking, a wide sweep of rolling hills covered with verdant grass. A few racehorses cantered by.

'You're right, Peter,' said Mum. 'It's stunning. A pity *that* spoils the view.'

That was Didcot, an industrial mess in the far distance.

'You're lucky up there,' he laughed. 'No Didcots on Mull. Just hills and sea. I loved it when we first went up there.'

'So come again,' she suggested. 'In the spring—before Anne gets too big to travel. I'd love to have you both up there.'

'So how about it?' he asked Anne.

'I'd like to go. Let me think about it. There's no rush.'

They finished the day with afternoon tea in Blewbury, a village of thatched cottages strung out along trickling streams. It was almost too chocolate boxy to be real. Again, Mum was amazed.

'I've never seen anything like it.'

'Prettier than Mull?' teased Peter.

Mum was a Scots loyalist to the core.

'Nearly,' she said. 'Nearly.'

Back home Mum cooked a light supper of scrambled eggs on toast, while Anne stuck to toast and honey. She had really enjoyed her day despite her mother going on about Dad, and she determinedly got out the wool and needles and made a few blue stitches. Then the phone rang.

'It's your girlfriend,' she snapped at Peter. '*Again.* Doesn't little Susan ever give up?'

'What does she want?'

'To talk to you, of course. She says "it's important".'

Peter had assumed that Susan was having a day's holiday, and so if she was calling him at home it must be really serious.

'Susan,' he asked. 'What on earth's the matter?'

She explained that she'd been to Cambridge and proudly told her story. Peter was amazed. He made her go over it twice to make sure he'd got it straight.

'Incredible!' he said. 'What a start! But how on earth does a death in the tennis clique in 1924 connect to contracts in 1963? *If at all.* It's one hell of a jump. We'll have to dig more. Well done, you *are* a clever girl. I'll see you on Monday. But what you've told me will keep my brain buzzing till then.'

'So what's keeping your brain buzzing?' snapped Anne. She had just heard the tail end of the conversation.

'What she's found out,' he replied. 'And by the way, she's not my girlfriend.'

'Your would-be girlfriend then. Don't tell me you don't fancy her.'

Peter decided to be objectively honest.

'If you weren't here, I might. But you *are* here, so I don't. Is that good enough?'

Anne looked straight at him, smiling broadly. 'That'll do for me.' She resumed her knitting with increased vigour.

Peter's brain buzzed all Saturday morning as they shopped in Maidenhead and all afternoon as he pathetically raked leaves off the lawn with his left hand, but nothing came. On Sunday Anne and Mum went to church, and in the afternoon they all went to Marlow where Anne proudly showed off her pictures. Mum was obviously enjoying herself, and so when Peter asked if she wanted to stay on, she needed no persuasion.

'But I must go on Wednesday. I'm chairing the Christmas fete committee on Friday, so I've got to be there.'

She cooked the supper, roast duck. Anne ate a bit, and it stayed down. Things were going well.

Peter left them to it on Monday, and got to work early. On his desk was a note.

'In food preparation room. Need the butter yellow.'

He took out his keys, unlocked the steel cabinet labelled "carcinogens" and took out three large bottles filled with intensely coloured liquid. He carefully put the bottles into a carrying crate and took the lift to the fifth floor.

In the preparation room, the noise of the grinder was intense. Rat food came in pellets, and so it had to be ground to a powder before the liquid carcinogen was mixed in. Susan waved as Peter arrived, but conversation was impossible until the grinder finished. When it did, they put on masks and gloves and tipped the powdered feed into a large bread mixer. Peter switched it on and carefully poured in the liquid, allowing it to mix for a full ten minutes and allowing them to talk over its quiet whir.

'I've been thinking about Cambridge all weekend,' he said. 'With no great effect. All we've really got is a death linked to the tennis clique which presumably included our precious two. Did they know John Napier? Is Napier related to the Master? And we don't even know if any of this is relevant. And if Lomax and Team didn't want to publicise their association, why on earth didn't they get rid of the photo? After all, they had 40 years to do it. I know it wouldn't have altered the official records, but it would have made their association less public.'

Susan spoke thoughtfully, selecting her words. 'Maybe Doctor Team didn't feel guilty about their association until now.'

Peter stared at her. 'Brilliant, Susan. Brilliant. I hadn't thought of *that.*'

He sat in silence for almost a minute as the mixer whirred on. 'You'd better get back there, and stay at the Gazette until you find that report on the inquest. And look in the library for anything linking Napier with Lomax and Team. What day would be best for you?'

'I think Thursday.'

'An appropriate day,' said Peter. 'That's when we decide about the contracts.'

The mixer finished its task, and they tipped the moist powder into the pelleting machine. Peter turned it on and it started to spit out tiny brown pellets which clattered into the feed hopper. They would be fed to the mice for three weeks to induce cancer and then the animals would be returned to their normal diet. Every two weeks over the next six months a proportion of the mice would be killed and their organs, particularly the livers, would be examined for tumours. All cancerous tissue would be analysed for its butter yellow content in a joint project between Peter and the Biochemistry Department to find out exactly how butter yellow induced cancer. When the pelleting was finished the room and equipment were carefully cleaned; Peter always insisted on doing it himself because of the dangerous chemicals involved.

He had already decided that Susan shouldn't have all the fun and games and decided he'd like to be a detective too. He left Susan busily working in the lab and went directly to Somerset House. He knew the Master's date of birth, the 26th of March 1880, and so it was just a matter of looking for the birth certificate, which he found after an hour of searching. The parents were a Mr and Mrs Alan Napier of Redgrave House in Little Chalfont. Luckily they had kept the same address and in the 1891 census they were listed as living with two sons, Robert and Stephen Napier, so the Master had had a brother.

Peter's next step was to track the birth certificate of the tennis star John Napier. He assumed that in his final year the student would have been about 21, which meant he had been born in 1902. Again he was lucky, and after another hour of searching found the certificate which showed that the young man was the son of Stephen Napier—making him the nephew of the Master.

Susan was both amazed and confused by the discovery.

'We seem to be going forward and backwards,' she said. 'John Napier was apparently in Paris when his fiancée died. So how on earth do Lomax and Team fit into this?'

'That's up to you,' said Peter. 'Dig deep at the Gazette on Thursday, while I play my hand at the meeting of the Heads.'

He actually played his hand well. The only item for decision was the Thirsk contract. Lomax went through the finance, which everyone agreed was generous and all agreed that Ron Team should head the project if it went ahead. No one else had the time. Then Lomax brought up the subject of animal facilities.

'As I said before,' he said. 'We've found suitable accommodation in Clerkenwell and we need staff, quite a considerable number, on short-term contracts. I think, in the circumstances, that they should be under the operational control of Ron Team.'

Peter was affronted. 'What about McDonald? Surely a man of his experience should be in charge.'

Lomax tried a conciliatory approach. 'He has a lot on. We thought it best if this short-term testing should be headed by someone else.'

Peter stared straight at him, playing his ace. 'As you know, I have no problem with us doing testing, but I really think that McDonald, who knows all about it must be in charge. If not, I really *don't* think I can go along with it.'

The biochemist Deidre Pearce and surgeon Stephens agreed with him, and so Lomax had to concede. McDonald would be in overall command of all the animal facilities. When it came to voting the Thirsk motion was carried 4 to 2.

Afterwards Deirdre made her peace with Peter.

'Sorry Peter, I've been a bit of a cow over this. I don't want it to stop us working together.'

Peter laughed cheerfully. 'The only cows I know are in fields producing milk.'

'Still friends?'

'Never weren't.'

To the amusement of the other Heads she gave him a peck on the cheek.

Peter had got what he wanted. The testing would go ahead with the animal staff under McDonald's control. That meant he could get his spy in place.

As promised, he rang home. Anne was remarkably cheerful, saying she hadn't been sick and was getting on well without Mum. Peter was delighted, and wondered how Susan was getting on in Cambridge.

She too was doing rather well. She had spent another two hours at the Gazette office looking for anything about Laura Marshall, and found what she wanted in the July edition.

'Student Death an Accident

The inquest into the death of Miss Laura Marshall on April 11th last returned a verdict of accidental death. Miss Marshall was last seen at the college at about 9 pm on the previous evening when she said she was taking a walk down to the river to say 'goodbye' before she returned home the next day. The autopsy report said the body was unmarked, except for some splinters of wood in her left elbow. Similar splinters were found in the edge of a landing stage by the river and were consistent with an attempt to drag herself from the water. The presence of water in the lungs, and the condition of the lungs were consistent with death by drowning. Mr John Napier, Miss Marshall's fiancé was present at the proceedings and the coroner extended his sympathy to Mr Napier and to Miss Marshall's parents who were also present.'

Susan took out Peter's Leica and carefully photographed the article. Then she went outside and phoned the Fellow from a call box. He was amazed to hear from her.

'When you said you'd call me I thought you were giving me the brush off,' he said plaintively.

'How could you think that?' she replied, trying to keep the sarcasm from her voice. 'Could I use the library again,' and then she forced herself to continue with the bribe. 'I'll buy you a drink afterwards?'

He was up for it.

In the library Susan checked the records of the tennis club. John Napier had won the tournament in Paris on the Saturday evening preceding his fiancé's death, and so he couldn't have been present at the drowning. According to the list of alumni he had not made any contact with the college since he left it. She thanked the librarian and limped painfully to the Kings Arms.

'What on earth are you doing in Cambridge?' asked the Fellow.

'I'm doing some research into the 1920s,' she replied, with some truth.

After two Babychams and three hopeful pats on the knee she escaped, found a taxi and caught the train home. She did not ring Peter.

Next morning, they reviewed their progress. They were both amazed at the amount of new information that they had acquired but still couldn't make sense of it.

'We need to know if John Napier is involved in all of this,' said Peter. 'Or whether it's just our precious pair. We really need to track him down and talk to him. And that's a tall order. He might not be in England.'

'Wouldn't Somerset House be of any use?' asked Susan.

'Not really,' replied Peter. 'The only way we are going to find him is by looking through all the electoral registers, and that would take an eternity. Anyway, I've something else on my mind. Do you think your mother would like to work in the Institute? If she did, I could really lean on McDonald and get her a job at Clerkenwell. After all, he owes me a favour. Then we'd have someone to tell us exactly what's going on there. But it would be important that people didn't realise she's your mother. She could use her maiden name.'

Susan's face lit up. 'I'll ask her, I'm sure she'd be interested. Wow! Two spies in the family.'

They both laughed.

'You're right,' said Peter. 'And she would be as important as you, with her nose right in the animal testing. And when that's finished I'm sure I could get McDonald to keep her on upstairs.'

'So what about John Napier? Are we giving up on him?'

'Not at all. But it's going to be difficult. After all, he'd be in his sixties. He could be dead.'

Actually he wasn't, though the doctor had told him he'd got less than a year. At that moment John Napier, MA (Cantab.), was sitting in his armchair, looking out over the Hampshire fields and watching the rain pour down. It was a bleak scene, but he was smiling. You do that when you have your chance for revenge.

Chapter 6
Testing Times

Lomax had obviously got things well-organised, and by the next week the location of the new animal premises was formally announced, and the Heads and McDonald were invited to go to Clerkenwell to see them. Peter felt a cold shiver go up his spine as he stepped inside the factory, and he instinctively reached up and touched his damaged shoulder. He looked carefully at the wall where his two assailants had been working. There were no new sockets or any sign of electrical work, and the wall had received fresh coating of plaster. All the gantries and industrial clutter had been removed and the place looked spic and span. Even McDonald was impressed.

'It should be fine,' he said. 'It's bigger than I expected. We should have plenty of room unless the testing gets out of hand.' He and his assistant started measuring the area and working out how many animal cages they could fit in.

Ron Team was also on good form. He had some colour in his cheeks, and was looking forward to getting Janet back from hospital.

'They've been great,' he said. 'They took the drains out yesterday, and it just needs more time to let it all heal up. She's looking really well.'

Peter was genuinely delighted for him, and temporarily forgot the lies and the contracts. They walked round to the back of the building to see what was there and Peter noticed a separate door leading up to a self-contained flat.

'Is that ours?' he asked.

'I'm not sure. Thirsk have not decided what to do with it. We don't really need the space, so they may just leave it empty or rent it out. It used to belong to the factory manager. So, what do you think of it all?'

'It should do its job,' said Peter. 'The main thing is that Macdonald seems happy with it.'

McDonald was also happy at Peter's intervention during the meeting of the Heads; it had kept him in control of all the animal facilities and he was pathetically grateful. Peter now knew that getting Susan's mum in place shouldn't be a problem. He decided to act quickly, and rang her when he got back to the lab, and yes, she would be delighted to come in early to see the McDonald Empire.

'Shall we come together?' asked Susan.

'Yes, but arrive separately.'

Mrs Preston was just what Peter expected. Small, like Susan, and cautiously confident with a superb knowledge of animals. Luckily she did not resemble her daughter. She was impressed by the facilities and obviously keen on the job in prospect.

'I'm so grateful for you seeing me, Dr Stott,' she said. 'It's so nice to meet you after all this time. Susan's told me all about you. She just loves working in your Department.'

'She's a great asset to the Institute,' said Peter, rather pompously. 'And I'm sure you will be too.'

After she'd left Susan arrived, looking anxious.

'So how did you two get on?' she asked.

'She'll be fine.'

The details of the testing program were finalised. Ron Team would be in overall charge and any testing on the He-La cells would be done by one of his assistants working in Peter's Department. Attempts on the further purification of cytocide would be done by the Biochemistry department, and Susan would work there part-time trying to find a test that could measure the quantity of the drug in animal tissue. Three new animal technicians would be recruited directly after Christmas to learn their job on the fifth floor with McDonald before being transferred to Clerkenwell when the animal facilities were ready.

Christmas came and went. Janet Team came to the Institute party, looking surprisingly well, and Anne liked the sapphire pendant that Peter bought for her in Hatton Garden. She stuck rigidly to her diet, refusing Christmas pudding and wine while the sickness gradually subsided. Her figure filled out, her skin glowed and she looked radiant. Deirdre Pearce saw her at the Institute in her party dress.

'My God, Peter,' she said. 'She's absolutely stunning. You must get her pregnant again.'

Peter blushed. For a rare moment he was completely tongue tied.

Susan took the news of Anne's pregnancy calmly, and seemed pleased.

'I know you like a son,' she said. 'Fingers crossed.'

'Thank you, Susan,' he answered gratefully.

Throughout February Peter and Susan made huge efforts to locate Robert Napier, but with no success. They looked at the list of British military deaths during the war and found nothing. They talked about Napier constantly, but the one person they did not mention was the man who had attacked Peter. After his visits to Clerkenwell he kept remembering the man's face, and Susan was haunted by the memories of Cambridge, but in an unconscious silent accord they agreed not to talk about him.

Their failure to locate Napier forced Peter on to a new tack, and he sent Susan to Companies House to look into Thirsk, who were financing the project, and Ciencia, who owned the patent. There was nothing even slightly odd about Thirsk: they had a good track record in financing companies and were trying to muscle into the lucrative pharmaceutical industry. Ciencia, however, was more interesting. It was a small company with just two directors, the husband and wife team of Juan and Antonia Lopez. The husband was a Spanish biochemist, hence the name of Ciencia, and the company looked at traditional medicines of the Third World to find their active ingredients. They had patented two products, one a treatment for leprosy and a second for arthritis, and had sold the patents to larger companies. Cytocide was their latest product, extracted from prickly pear grown near Juan's native city of Cadiz.

Susan's mum was interviewed under her maiden name of Denise Locke. McDonald liked her, but was doubtful about her age and insisted that she was employed on a two month's trial rather than the usual four weeks, but after three weeks he was happy.

'You were right, Dr Stott,' he said. 'She really is very good indeed.'

Susan's only problem was remembering to call her mother Denise. She practised it at home and became word perfect. At the Institute they rarely came in contact because the animal staff took their breaks at different times than the laboratory staff, and the deception seemed to be working. She enjoyed the prospect of working with Deirdre Pearce, and was looking forward to doing some hardline biochemical research.

'Before we start to look for a test we need to make sure that cytocide is just one product and not a mixture,' said Deidre. 'I think that all the uncertainty about whether cytocide works or not may be caused by the fact that we haven't got it pure enough. I think we need to go back to basics, and that means getting some prickly pear to work on.'

'So where will we get it from?' asked Susan.

'We could get it from Spain, but I think an easier bet would be Kew Gardens. They've got some growing in their greenhouses. I'll talk to their research director and see if we can acquire some. He owes me a favour.'

She was as good as her word. Two weeks later two large plants were installed in a brilliantly lit small greenhouse in the corner of the laboratory, and Deirdre outlined her research strategy to Susan.

'We know cytocide contains sulphur,' she said. 'So theoretically, if we put radioactive sulphate in the nutrient mix it will end up in the cytocide and it will give us a marker to see if it's just one molecule or a mixture. There could be two or more forms of cytocide, both containing sulphur, but I hope not. That would really confuse things. So would you like to help us out on this?'

'Yes please.'

'Then I'll talk to Peter. I'm sure it will be okay. By the way, have you worked with radioisotopes before?'

'No.'

'Well, sulphur 35 isn't the best one to start with. It's a hard beta emitter, so it's easy to count, but you have to be careful with it. The radiation isn't strong enough to go through thick glass, so an ordinary test-tube will give you protection. You just have to make sure you don't get it *in* you or *on* you. You'll have to work really tidily, and you'll need a radiation badge.'

Team was theoretically in charge of all isotope use in the Institute, and so Deirdre and Peter had to brief him about the experiment.

'Sounds interesting,' he said, without enthusiasm. 'Keep me posted on how you're getting on.'

Peter and Deirdre exchanged glances, and Deirdre made the approach.

'So how are things?' she asked cautiously.

Team was waiting to be asked. 'Not good. In fact, about as bad as they could be. Janet's got pain in her side. They've done a biopsy, and found a secondary in the liver.' He paused, his face drawn. 'You both know the score with that.'

They did indeed. It meant months, possibly weeks. Deirdre pressed Team's shoulder and gave him a comforting pat on the back.

'I'm so sorry Ron. Truly sorry.'

Peter was genuinely appalled. You wouldn't wish *that* on your worst enemy.

'Dear God, Ron. Poor you, poor Janet. I can't imagine what you're going through. If there's anything I can do.'

'Just pray,' said Ron pathetically. 'Just pray, like me. And hope for a miracle.'

The work had to go on and so Deirdre ordered the radioisotope from Harwell, and the two plants were moved into the radioisotope lab. Extra lighting and heating was installed, the benches were covered with waterproof paper and the experiment was scheduled to start in early March. The animal testing programme also started at almost the same time, and Susan's mum was moved permanently to Clerkenwell. This was a great relief to Susan, who had found it difficult avoiding contact with her mother while they were together at the Institute. From now on it would be easy, they could travel in together, but Susan's mum had either to remember to get off the Tube at Chancery Lane or to change at Liverpool Street and go on to Farringdon.

The box containing the radioactive sulphur was surprisingly large. In the middle of the packing was a sealed tin can which could have contained peaches. Using thick gloves, Deidre opened the can with a conventional tin opener and extracted a small lead cylinder which she put behind the thick glass screen on the bench. Working extremely carefully she prised off the lid of the cylinder and extracted a small glass ampoule containing a clear liquid.

'Is that it?' asked Susan excitedly. 'Doesn't look like much.'

'Sure is. This is the tricky bit.'

With a fine pair of pliers Deirdre peeled back the aluminium seal on the ampoule to reveal a rubber injection port on the top. She fitted a needle to a glass syringe, drove it through the rubber port and carefully sucked up the liquid which she then squirted into a beaker of cactus growth medium. She stirred the medium with a glass rod.

'Mission accomplished,' she said. 'Now for the feeding.'

With extreme care she poured the growth medium into a measuring cylinder and poured half of it into each of the flower pots containing the prickly pear. Finally she put all the contaminated glassware behind a thick glass screen at the end of the bench.

'Watch,' she said. She pointed the Geiger counter through the glass screen directly at the prickly pear. There was almost no reading. Then she put her hand behind the screen and held the counter directly over the top of one of the plants. The Geiger screamed.

'That's it,' said Deidre. 'Your lesson of the day. Keep the glass between you and the stuff you're working with and you're safe as houses. Get it on you and you're in trouble. But don't worry, we'll be working together.'

'How long shall we leave it before we start to extract the cytocide?' asked Susan.

'I don't really know, but we've got to get as much radiation into the cytocide as possible. I did think a couple of days, but on reflection I think we will give it a week. So I think you need to get set up ready for a Tuesday start.'

The equipment needed to extract the cytocide was moved into the lab. There was a huge blender sufficient to mash up all the flesh of the prickly pear, and all the chemicals and glassware needed to do the extraction according to the procedure detailed in the Ciencia patent. Susan had studied the method and was worried about its complexity.

'Don't worry,' said Deidre, reassuring her once again. 'I'll be working with you.'

Susan took the morning setting up the isotope laboratory and then went back to see Peter. As she had spare time on her hands she expected to be put again on the search for the elusive Napier, but Peter had other ideas.

'We're just amateurs,' he said.' We've done all we can and got absolutely nowhere. I think it's time for some professionals.'

'Professionals?'

'Private detectives. I've been thinking about it for some time. A friend of mine used some in Birmingham to get evidence in a court case. He said they were good, efficient, and discreet.'

Susan was amazed. The only private detectives she knew were in her favourite American crime fiction.

'Don't private eyes cost a lot?' she asked.

'Yes,' said Peter. 'They do indeed. But I've got some money in a Post Office savings account which should be enough.'

Susan looked straight at him, her eyes posing the question.

'No,' he said.' I'm not going to tell Anne. This is our secret. There's an oncology meeting at Birmingham University in a fortnight. You know that, you helped do the slides. So while I'm there I'll go and see our private eyes and get things going. You can come too, if you want. I didn't ask you before because of what happened at the last conference.'

Susan was too excited to be worried about Cambridge.

'So what are they called, these private eyes?' she asked. Her eyes were sparkling. She was expecting something glamorous like Philip Marlowe or Mickey Spillane.

'Lawrences, it's run by two cousins of the same name. Come along and meet them with me. You should have finished the extraction by then. If not I am sure Deidre will give you a day off.'

'Thank you Peter. That will be my treat.'

The actual Ciencia patent was based on the extraction of 100 kg of fresh prickly pear. Susan hoped to get about two kilograms of tissue from their two rather small plants, and so she had scaled down the quantities in the patent by a factor of 50. Working with very thick rubber gloves Deidre cut the plants into pieces with a knife and Susan weighed them directly into the huge glass blender. She added two litres of water, pressed the switch, and the pear dispersed into a green soup which she poured into a huge beaker. She added an equal volume of alcohol and stirred the mixture with a glass rod. The colour changed to a dirty white and Susan put the glass screen in front of the beaker.

'So now we leave it for an hour,' she said. 'Then we filter it.'

'That's it,' reflected Deidre. 'We leave it for whatever time it takes to settle out. I think that 99% of the radioactivity will be in the liquid. So when you've filtered it you'll be working on the solid which should only have about 300 microcuries in it, a hell of a comedown from the three millicuries we started with. So the nasty bit will be over.'

After the hour there was a mass of white sludge on the bottom of the beaker. Susan carefully siphoned off the clear liquid above the sludge and poured it into an enormous glass carboy under the bench. All the liquids used in the extraction would be stored for at least six months until the radiation in them had declined enough to allow them to be poured down the drain.

Susan spent the next two days completing the extraction procedure. She worked very carefully, making sure that she understood each step in the process, and so only once did she need Deidre's help. The sludge was filtered out with a suction pump and then dried out in pure alcohol. Then came the main procedures, a series of extractions with ether and benzene, and the final product was a minute coating of a white cytocide at the bottom of the extraction flask. Deirdre was called in to see it, and she instantly put the Geiger counter over the top of the flask. To her relief the meter clicked frantically.

'Wow,' she chortled. 'Well done Susan. There's plenty of radioactivity there, it's about as good as we could have hoped for.'

Susan felt a huge glow of pride. The extraction had really gone well.

'Tomorrow it will be the chromatography,' said Deidre. 'Unknown territory. That's when it should get interesting.'

Chromatography was the new "in" technique. It gave biochemists the ability to separate mixtures of very similar substances, and Susan would be using it for the first time. Deirdre had had the chromatography tube made in plastic rather than glass so that they could monitor any radiation inside it. Plastic, unlike glass, did not stop the beta radiation. The long plastic tube, which had a tap on the bottom end, was clamped vertically and filled with tiny globules of a brown resin which Deidre hoped would absorb the radioactive cytocide. The small amount of powder Susan had extracted from the prickly pear was mixed into 10 millilitres of water and two millilitres of that was pipetted onto the top of the column of resin in the tube. She opened the tap slightly, the liquid sank into the resin, and Deirdre added some more water. All the liquid dripping through the tap at the bottom of the chromatography tube was monitored for radioactivity. There was none. Deirdre pointed the Geiger counter at the top inch of the resin column and the meter clicked furiously.

'First success,' she said delightedly. 'All the cytocide is definitely absorbed on to the resin.'

'And now?' asked Susan.

'We've got to get the cytocide *off* the resin,' said Deidre. 'We could use acid, but that would damage the cytocide. We'll start by putting through various concentrations of salt and see if the cytocide comes off as a whole or in two or more components. We've got enough radiocytocide for four more goes.'

It took almost a week of painstaking work before they had any success. At their fourth attempt they managed to remove almost one third of the radioactivity on the column with a 4.5% solution of salt. The rest came off with a 5% solution, leaving nothing on the resin. Deirdre was ecstatic.

'That's it then. Cytocide is a mixture of at least two things. So this brings out a new problem. Which of the two forms of cytocide has any anti-cancer activity? Either? Both? Or do they work together? Now we've opened up a real new can of worms. Ron Team will be fascinated by all this.'

'Do you have to tell him?' asked Susan carefully.

'Of course I'll tell him.' Deirdre was shocked by Susan's disloyalty. 'Why ever not, Susan?'

'I just thought we should repeat the experiment first,' replied Susan lamely.

'Of course we'll do it a second time.' Deidre's reply was crushing. 'That's what we scientists *do*.'

So they did it all again, with the same result, and Deirdre reported it to Team.

'What about Thirsk?' asked Susan. 'Do we tell them as well?'

'No,' said Deidre. 'Certainly not yet. I didn't want anything to do with this testing, you know that. I'm doing this radioactivity thing on my own bat because it could be useful to the Institute in the future. Thirsk aren't paying us for it. My paid job is to find a reliable test for cytocide and to report to them if and when I've done it.'

Susan updated Peter with the progress on cytocide as they sat on the train to Birmingham. He was intrigued by the results, and worried that Deirdre had passed them to Ron Team.

'I don't like that bastard knowing too much,' he snarled. 'I don't trust him. I used to, he was my friend. Not anymore. I'm just sorry for Janet with the cancer.'

Susan was startled by his unusual venom.

'But we've still got our spy in his camp,' she said soothingly.

'Oh yes, and how's Denise—your mum getting on?'

'Fine. They've really got going. But she is amazed by the anonymity of it all. They're told to inject and feed the animals, but they've no idea what they're injecting or what's in the food. All the raw data from the dissections and weighing goes directly to Dr Team for analysis.'

'That sounds like the standard double-blind experimental program,' explained Peter. 'It's standard practice. The FDA, the Federal Drug Administration, insists on it. It stops the workers consciously or unconsciously biasing the results.'

'Yes, of course.'

'Sorry I snapped,' apologised Peter. 'You don't need to look worried, I was only cross at Team.'

'It's not that,' she admitted. 'I am just praying that that dreadful Fellow from Mark's won't be at the conference.'

Peter grinned. 'I can assure you, my dear Miss Preston, that the love of your life will not be there. I've checked the list of delegates. So relax.'

'Thank God for that,' she said fervently, and switched her thoughts to the private detectives they would be meeting. According to Susan's crime novels, the offices of private eyes were untidy, dirty, with full ashtrays and a smell of bourbon. These offices were nothing like that. The Birmingham office was immaculately clean and tidy, as were the Lawrences; two small smartly dressed men who exuded charm and confidence. Peter particularly liked their directness.

'As you know, Dr Stott, we have only been working for two years now and so we have to make our reputation,' said the older one. 'You need results, and in return we will charge you on that basis. Our rates are expenses plus fifteen shillings per hour—paid as we go, on a monthly basis. When we get the results you want there will be a final additional charge of a further fifteen shillings per hour.'

Thirty bob an hour, thought Peter incredulously, *that's not far off from what I get.*

'Give me a minute to think,' he said to the cousins, but he knew instinctively that the offer of payment by results had won him over. 'Okay. I'm convinced. I've had good reports about you and you've got all of Napier's details. So where do I sign?'

'Here, please, Dr Stott.'

After that the conference went well. Peter did a short presentation which was well received, while Susan watched admiringly. He was right: her Cambridge would-be lover wasn't there and so she could relax and enjoy the experience of chatting to world experts. To her delight she found that she was getting better at holding her own, and so on the train home she was unusually relaxed and assertive.

'So how's Anne?' she asked.

Peter was intrigued. Prior to Anne's pregnancy Susan had rarely asked about his wife, but now she wanted to know everything, often asking what she had already asked before.

'She's fine. But she's getting really big now. We've got a cot, and we've decorated the nursery.'

'What colour?'

'Oxford blue, what else?'

'So you're still hoping for a boy?'

'Oh yes. We both want a son.'

'So what about a name?'

'Michael.'

'That's nice,' she said, smiling cheerfully. 'My dad was a Michael. But suppose it's a girl?'

Peter grinned back. 'Then I suppose it'll have to be Michaela.'

Susan kept the interrogation going. 'And how about the trip to Scotland next month. Is it still on?'

'I don't think so,' said Peter. 'Anne doesn't feel like it. But her mum is coming down to help out when the baby arrives.'

'So you'll be here through April?' Susan got to the point at last. 'It's just that I wanted—' she hesitated. 'My lecturer says that my electrochemistry isn't up to scratch and that I need some help with it.' She hesitated again. 'I wondered if you would do it? I don't have the money for a private tutor and I can't ask Deirdre and the finals are in May.'

'Of course,' said Peter with some asperity. 'Why on earth didn't you ask me before? We don't want you failing on some obscure point. I'll bone up on it for you.'

'Thank you so much, Peter.'

Peter dug out his old tome on electrochemistry and read it conscientiously on the train to work the next day. Hell fire, he'd forgotten most of it, and he knew a lot of revision was in order. When he got to the Institute he put the subject out of his head and concentrated on the meeting he was having with Deirdre Pearce.

'What we really need,' she said rather bossily, 'is to separate a large amount of cytocide into its two components and test each for its anti-cancer properties. All we need is a lot of cytocide and a huge resin column. But before we do that we need to have a *test* for cytocide in both its forms so that we can monitor what is happening during the chromatography. That has to be our priority.'

Peter had no problem with that.

'Absolutely. You're right. It's essential. If we do it we'll get the money from Thirsk and we'll also be able to push our personal research along. So go for it. You can have Susan as long as you want.'

'Fine,' said his colleague. 'I like her and she works hard. Thanks, Peter.'

During the next three months Peter concentrated on the forthcoming birth of their first child. The midwife was concerned that the baby seemed unduly large, and so Peter insisted on Anne seeing an obstetrician.

'It's as we both thought, Mrs Stott,' he said. 'The baby is big, and you are small, but I've delivered larger babies from smaller women. So there shouldn't be any problem.'

Anne's eyes went wet with relief. 'So I won't need a Caesarean.'

'I never say never, Mrs Stott. But it's unlikely.'

'Thank you, Doctor.' Anne shook his hand and wiped the tears from her eyes. 'I just didn't want my son cut out of me while I'm unconscious. I want to see him *first.*'

The two men were amazed at her vehemence, and the obstetrician soothed her down.

'And I'm sure you will, Mrs Stott. I'm sure you will.'

Peter and Anne celebrated the good news with dinner and a bottle of Chablis, and Peter stopped worrying. It was all going to be okay. In April he also concentrated on Susan's problem. He had finally made himself reasonably expert on electrochemistry and insisted that Susan had a twice weekly tutorial with him in the Institute library.

'A little and often,' he said. 'We'll keep it up till your exam, and you'll sail through in May.'

Summer came and it got hot. Anne sat in the garden, relaxing by painting and keeping cool, while Peter rang up regularly to see how she was. She had a false alarm near her due date and Peter took a week off work to be with her. The actual birth was easy and uncomplicated, and Peter had only to stay two hours in the waiting room before the nurse called him in.

Anne was sitting up in bed, a small bundle at her breast. She beamed at Peter and gave him the thumbs up.

'Come and meet Michael,' she said proudly. 'Michael, meet your Dad.'

Peter put his arm around her and rested his head on hers. His tears flooded down on to her face, mixed with hers and dripped down on to Michael, who stirred in protest. They laughed. They cried again. They were happy.

The next three months were also the happiest of Peter's life. He enjoyed being a father, he enjoyed watching his son beginning to develop human characteristics, and he was glad to see Anne so content and fulfilled. Michael was no trouble: he cried for food, suckled his milk and then went back to sleep. Mum had come down from Scotland when she got Peter's telegram and she was delighted with her grandson.

'He's so beautiful,' she said. 'Blue eyes and brown hair.'

'And he looks just like Anne,' groaned Peter in mock horror. 'Not a trace of me.'

Mum laughed. 'Sorry, Peter. Family resemblances run strong with us. You didn't stand a chance. But I'm sure he'll be as bright as his dad.'

With Mum settled in at Maidenhead Peter went back to work where everyone was pleased to see him. Deirdre Pearce gave him a congratulatory hug and Susan was keen to hear all the details.

'He was eight pounds and four ounces,' said Peter proudly, 'and born at 9:20 in the morning of June the 30th. Anne is fine, she's really enjoying being a mother.'

'I'm really pleased,' said Susan. 'I'm glad it's a boy and that he's a Michael. By the way.' She looked aside to make sure no one was listening. 'Any news from Birmingham?'

Peter shrugged. 'The last two letters were negative, or to be exact rather expensive negatives. But I'll keep going. Anyway, what about you? Any exam news?'

'No,' she said. 'Still waiting, fingers crossed. Another thing. Dr Team wants to talk to you.'

The last thing Peter wanted to do was to talk to his ex-friend, but Team tracked them down in the cafeteria at lunchtime. He looked unusually bright and cheerful.

'Congratulations Peter, well done indeed. I hear Anne and baby are doing well.'

'Thanks Ron.' Peter forced himself to be pleasant and concerned. 'How are things?'

As before, Team had been waiting to be asked. 'Much better than I could have dreamed of. Janet's stopped losing weight. In fact she started to gain. And she's needing less morphine.'

Even Peter had to be pleased at that. 'A bloody miracle,' he said. 'Good for her. I'm so happy for you both.'

'You're right,' said Ron with a smile. 'A bloody miracle.'

'We need a miracle around here,' said Susan after Ron had left. 'We need to find some answers as to what's going on. Then things will get better.'

In fact things were to get very much worse. The events which were to shake the Institute to its very foundations were triggered just a few weeks later, and were revisited at the subsequent trial at the Old Bailey the following year. As was customary, the Queens Counsel for the prosecution opened the proceedings.

'Ladies and gentlemen of the jury. The chain of events which I am about to outline, which culminated in an orgy of violence and criminality, began with the suspicions of a certain Miss Susan Preston and her mother Mrs Denise Preston on the 10th of October 1964. As you will hear in the subsequent evidence, both of these ladies were working at that time at the Marshall Institute for Cancer Research.'

Susan hadn't heard the QCs opening statement. She'd been sitting in the witness room, waiting to be called, and mentally gearing herself up for the ordeal ahead. It was there in her head, every awful detail.

The trail had begun months back when Deirdre had been devising her test for cytocide, a procedure which had involved coupling the cytocide with a diazo dye to produce a blue colour. The only trouble was that it wasn't sensitive enough, as Deirdre had explained.

'At the moment we can only detect cytocide at the level of one milligram per litre. But to detect it in biological samples we need a sensitivity one hundred times greater, and we're nowhere near that.'

So they'd persevered, changing the reaction conditions and refining their techniques, and finally, on the Friday before Deirdre was due to go to a conference they thought they'd nearly cracked it. Susan had gone home that weekend in a state of high excitement, and the following Monday she'd followed Deirdre's new instructions and, to her delight, the sensitivity had increased to the required level. They'd nearly got there.

On the Tuesday she'd asked a technician to prepare five solutions of cytocide without telling her the exact concentrations. She had analysed his solutions, and the concentrations she'd calculated exactly matched his. Mission accomplished.

As she sat in the lab congratulating herself on her success, Susan's thoughts had suddenly switched to detection. Peter had got her mother the job at Clerkenwell as a potential spy, and now it had seemed time to activate her. What was happening at Clerkenwell had been a closely guarded secret; the actual amount of cytocide being injected or fed to the animals had been known only by Thirsk, Ron Team and the Head of the Institute, and now there seemed to be a real opportunity to find out what was going on. To that end she'd rung Clerkenwell.

'Hello, is that you, Denise?'

'Yes.'

'Can you talk Mum?' Susan had asked anxiously. 'Anyone around?'

'No, they are all out the back.'

'Mum. I need a favour. I want you to bring home a couple of the samples of cytocide solution that you've been injecting. A few millilitres of each will do.'

'All right,' Mum had said doubtfully. 'But what are you going to do with them?'

'Check the levels of cytocide.'

On the Wednesday morning Susan had analysed the two samples and to her disbelief neither solution had contained any detectable cytocide. No blue colour, nothing, and so she had repeated the tests, and, to her incredulity they had remained negative. She had been perplexed rather than concerned— possibly Mum had brought home two control samples which would not have contained any drug, and so she'd rung her mother again.

'Mum. This is important, really important.'

'What is?'

'Listen Mum. I need you to keep samples of all the solutions you injected today.'

'That's 12 samples,' her mother said doubtfully.

'Just do it Mum,' Susan had been unusually forceful. 'I'll come over at lunchtime and collect them.'

Later that afternoon Susan analysed the samples one by one. The first had contained no cytocide, as did the second one, and by the 12th negative result Susan was shaking with apprehension and worry. What the hell was going on? She had desperately needed help from someone she could trust, but Deirdre was in Dublin and Peter was in Scotland. So she'd rung her mother again, an act that she would regret for the rest of her life.

'Mum, I don't believe this. None of your solutions had any cytocide in them.'

A stunned silence.

'That can't be right Susan. You must have made a mistake.'

'But I haven't Mum. I've checked and checked.'

'Are you telling me that all the time I've been working here I've just been injecting saline?' Her mother's voice had had a shriek of disbelief. 'I don't believe it. Why would anyone do that?'

'I don't know Mum. I really don't. Something is really, really wrong. It stinks.'

'So what do we do now?'

'Nothing,' Susan had said firmly. 'Not anything at all. We must keep quiet until Peter gets back on Monday. Say absolutely nothing to anyone'

Chapter 7
Men of Action

Mr Alan Jones was a stalwart of the Ilford community. He was a town councillor as well as the chairman of the local gardening club, and nothing really exciting had ever happened to him. He had always wondered what he would do in an emergency. Could he cope? Would he do the right thing? The events that early Sunday morning answered those questions for him, and gave him enough stories to bore his gardening colleagues to death for the next two years.

He was in the front garden with his secateurs when he saw the women approaching. They stopped to admire the scent of his late climbing rose, and he was so pleased that he cut off a flower for each of them. He was turning to hand over the flowers when he saw the car. It was travelling at normal speed down the road, but suddenly it accelerated and swung up the pavement. It made no effort to stop, its wing scraping along his front wall and allowing no escape for its victims. He screamed out a warning, throwing himself backwards and landing badly on his ankle. As he lay there he saw the bodies of the older woman and her dog flip over the car bonnet while the body of the younger one was forced through his gate. Painfully he crawled to the first body. She had landed head first on the wall, and her dog lay dead beside her, still pathetically attached to his dead mistress by its lead. Both bodies twitched, but Alan knew there was no hope. He struggled over to the girl. Bone projected through her shin, and blood was pouring out. He ripped off his belt, wrapped it around her thigh, and tightened the tourniquet with the handle of his secateurs. Only then did he yell out to his wife.

'For God's sake, Jo, call an ambulance. And the police.'

She just couldn't do it; she came to the front door and screamed hysterically at the carnage on her front lawn, and so it was a neighbour who had to make the phone call.

Peter arrived home from Scotland the next morning. Anne and he had enjoyed their trip to Mull, and Mum had been delighted to see them and show off her grandson. Things had gone so well that Anne had decided to stay on another few days, and so only Peter had taken the sleeper south that Saturday evening. The train had stopped and started throughout the night and he hadn't slept at all, and he wished he'd taken a sleeping pill. It was also an hour and a half late. At Paddington he phoned Johnson's, the local minicab in Maidenhead and they were there when he arrived at the station.

There were letters on the mat as he opened the front door, and he picked them up and stacked them on the kitchen table. After a black coffee he opened them, leaving the one with the week old Birmingham postmark till last. Peter assumed it was yet another negative reply from the agency, and was seriously considering how much longer he could waste money with them. He could not have been more wrong.

Dear Dr Stott,

At last some good news. I think we have definitely traced John Napier for you. My brother in Australia is in the same business as me, and I asked him to look to see if any Ron Napier served in the Australian services during the war. He struck lucky. Mr Napier served in the Japanese campaign and was badly wounded. He had apparently immigrated to Australia just after the First World War. He was married, but his wife died recently and he returned to England so that he could be near his daughter. She is married and living over here. His address is 6, Long Lane, Farleigh Wallop, which is a village outside Basingstoke in Hampshire.

If you need any more information please let us know.

All best wishes,

John Lawrence

Peter sat there, grinning with delight, and suddenly remembered Susan. She ought to know the good news. He phoned her, but there was no reply. Worn out from the journey, he went upstairs for a nap and overslept till early afternoon. When he tried Susan's number again a male voice answered.

'This is the Essex police. Can I help you?'

'I was trying to get hold of Susan—' said Peter. As he said it he knew that something was seriously wrong. 'What's happened?'

'And who are you, sir?'

'I am Dr Stott,' he said.' Susan works for me, and I wanted to tell her some news.'

'Sorry, Dr Stott, but there's been an accident. Miss Preston has been badly injured, and her mother is dead.'

Peter felt his knees buckling under him, and he slid onto a chair. For a moment he thought he was going to faint.

'Dr Stott, are you still there?'

'Yes, I'm here. Sorry, it was a hell of a shock. What happened?'

'They were both run down by a car in Ilford early this morning. The driver didn't stop. Dr Stott, I have to ask you this. Can you think of anyone who would want to harm the Prestons? We have a very good witness who says categorically that the car was driven at them deliberately. If so we are dealing with murder.'

Peter could feel a cold sweat on his brow. 'No,' he said instinctively. 'I can't think of anyone. Have you spoken to Susan?'

'No we can't at the moment, but we will. At the moment she is undergoing surgery to repair her right leg.'

'And where is she?'

'She is in St Thomas's in London, in the orthopaedic unit. Dr Stott, can I—?'

Peter put the receiver down, and grabbed the car keys. It was Sunday, so the traffic was light, and he got to the hospital by late afternoon. There were two policemen idling in the corridor outside a small room, so he knew where Susan was.

'Is she out of the theatre?' asked Peter anxiously, addressing the older of the two policemen. 'I'm Dr Stott, I may have spoken to one of you on the phone this afternoon.'

'That was me, sir.'

'I'm sorry I cut you off,' apologised Peter. 'I was so shocked and worried.'

'I think you can ease off the worrying, sir. By the way, I am Inspector Grey. The surgeons say she will recover, but there will be a lot of scarring. At the moment we're waiting for her to come round. It would be nice if you could be here for that, a friendly face.'

'Of course I will. That's what I am here for. Oh God, I didn't bring any flowers.'

'I am sure she won't be worrying about that, sir. Bring some next time. And by the way, did you think of anyone wanting to harm them? I know I asked you this before.'

'No,' said Peter. 'I can't think of anyone.'

'No jealous boyfriend?'

'No boyfriend at all that she's mentioned.'

'Just some routine, Dr Stott, please. Where were you at about eleven this morning?'

'I was having a nap. I just got back from Scotland at about half past ten.'

'Can anyone confirm that?'

Peter thought slowly. 'Oh yes,' he said. 'Johnson's minicab picked me up at the station at twenty past ten. They'll confirm it. We use them a lot.'

'Do you have their address? Or their telephone number?'

Peter fished in his pocket, pulled out the taxicab card and handed it over.

The police man seemed satisfied. 'You can go in if you want, sir.'

It was much worse than Peter expected. Susan's right leg was in traction, suspended by a series of pulleys and weights, and blood dripped steadily into a tube in her arm, but it was her face that shocked him. Her right cheek was black with bruises and was stitched. Peter counted the black knots on her face. Dear God, there were six. Her eyes had sunk into her puffed face and his pretty assistant had been reduced to a slab of butcher's meat. He sat down beside her and took her hand, and she stirred at his touch and managed to whisper through her swollen lips.

'Peter, it's you. What are you doing here?' She gazed vaguely around and then dozed off. A few minutes later she drifted back into consciousness. 'Oh, I remember, I've got something to tell you. Mum and I agreed that we must keep it quiet until we saw you.' She explained with agonised difficulty what had happened in Clerkenwell.

Peter sat in shocked amazement, getting his thoughts together while his logical brain kicked in. 'And you told no one about it?'

'No, no one.'

He sat still, holding her hand, watching her slip in and out of consciousness. He could feel tears pricking his eyes and a cold rage rising inside him. He'd felt guilt when Susan had been hurt in Clerkenwell, but now he was overwhelmed by it. She struggled back to wakefulness.

'What's happened, Peter?'

'There was a car accident with you and your mum. You're in hospital here in London.'

'And Mum?'

His face said it all. She gazed at him long and hard, then turned her face into the pillow and sobbed. Peter stayed with her, his tears gone and his eyes like stones. The Prestons had discovered either incompetence or wrongdoing in the testing programme, and days later they had been mown down by a car. Someone had to pay. He didn't know who that someone was, but he knew that the man who was key to it all lived near Basingstoke

'Did she say anything?' asked the detective.

'She asked about her mother,' said Peter.' And I couldn't lie, I had to tell her. I don't think she's up to answering any questions. I'm sorry, but she did ask.'

'Are you off now sir?'

'Yes, but I'll come back tomorrow. I'll ring back tonight to see if she's making progress.'

Peter drove home slowly, thinking hard as he went. The AA guide told him that Farleigh Wallop was just south of Basingstoke, and he wondered whether he should drive down immediately and confront Napier, but he was exhausted and so he decided against it and went home instead. Inside he phoned the hospital, who said that Susan was "making fair progress".

He arrived in Farleigh Wallop just before eight the next morning, and with some difficulty found Napier's scruffy bungalow just outside the village. He knew the MG was conspicuous, so he parked it behind a hedge some way out and walked into the village in hiking gear. He wore driving gloves, and had his father's old truncheon in his rucksack. The bungalow was typical of the 1930s, with a four sectioned roof rising to a point in the centre. The garden was unkempt, and a rusty spade stood against the ageing conservatory. The milkman had just left a bottle on the step, and Peter saw movement behind the conservatory door. As it opened he spoke to the figure.

'Mr Napier? Mr John Napier?'

The grey-haired man answered. 'Yes, that's me.'

'Then I'd like to talk to you about drug testing and Ciencia.'

Bull's eye. The man underwent what the police would call an intense visible reaction.

'I don't know anything about it. Who the hell are you?'

'My name is Peter Stott. I work at MICR where Ciencia is testing out cytocide. Some of the animal work is being done incorrectly.'

'I don't know anything about animals,' said Napier sullenly.

'But you must know about the fake results.'

Napier went red.

'You can either talk to me,' continued Peter relentlessly. 'Or you can talk to the police. It's your choice. But you'll talk.'

Napier shrugged. 'You'd better come in.'

He turned and shuffled slowly down the grimy corridor into the equally grimy sitting room and sat on the solitary armchair. Peter took the sofa.

'Second chance,' he said. 'Tell me about Ciencia.'

'I'm damned if I will,' said the old man defiantly.

Peter had to admire his guts. He took out the truncheon and tapped it on Napier's knee.

Napier's face went ashen. He was shaking, but still defiant.

'So kill me,' he whispered. 'I'm dying anyway. If I'm dead you won't get anything from me.'

Peter changed tactics.

'Now listen. And listen damned carefully. A friend of mine has been murdered because of you, and another friend has been badly injured. So talk. It's your choice. You'll have to talk to the police or you can talk to me. It's up to you.'

To his surprise and admiration Napier actually became angry.

'Sure I know about Ciencia,' he hissed. 'But I don't know anything about your bloody murder. I'm not a bloody killer, *they* bloody are.'

Peter remembered his interrogation training in the Army. *A guilty subject will scream and cry if accused, the non-guilty will get angry.*

'So who are *they*?'

'Those swine, Lomax and Team.' Napier clutched his chest. 'Jesus, it hurts. Christ.' His face was going blue, and he was sweating profusely. He took a capsule out of his pocket, broke it, and held it under his nose.

It was a close call for almost five minutes, and Peter prayed that Napier wouldn't die before he talked, but slowly and surely his colour came back and his hand dropped from his chest. He was going to live, thank God.

'Angina,' he whispered eventually. 'Forgot to take my pills.'

Peter went into the kitchen, selected two cups from the pile of filthy crockery, washed them carefully and made tea for both of them. Back in the sitting room he handed Napier his drink.

'Fine,' he said quietly. 'I hate those two as much as you, and I do believe you when you said you had nothing to do with the killing. But I'm pretty sure Ciencia must be involved in it. I can only decide that if you tell me the truth. And I need to know where Lomax and Team fit into all this. I admire your loyalty to Ciencia, but if they caused the killings your loyalty goes. You know that.'

For the next few minutes Napier sat in silence, sipping his tea. Then he sighed.

'Okay. Where do you want me to start?'

'At the beginning. Start with the girl in the river at Cambridge. Start with Laura Marshall.'

The old man's face lit up, and he smiled longingly. 'So you know about her. Laura was the love of my life, you know. You never forget your first love. And when I got back from Paris she was dead.'

Peter said nothing, and Napier struggled on.

'At the inquest they said she'd drowned, and I believed them. After that I couldn't stand England, so I went off to Australia to try my luck. There I got married to Elaine and we had a daughter, just before war broke out. The Japs took me prisoner in

Singapore. Bastards. I never recovered from it. But I did make some money afterwards and did quite well. Then Elaine died and I came back to England to be near my daughter. She lives here.'

Napier stopped to draw breath and collect his thoughts.

'I happened to be near Cambridge one day, so I thought I'd go back to see the place. Lay those ghosts, so to speak. So I called in on my uncle. He was very ill, dying. At first he seemed shocked to see me, then he seemed glad. Then he got very upset, saying that something had happened in the past, something bad, something that involved me. He finally got so upset that he couldn't speak and said he'd write me a letter about it all. I was totally confused, but as he was so ill I didn't push it. Then about six weeks later I got a letter from his solicitor, saying that he had died and enclosing a letter from him to me. And you know what was in it?'

Napier's voice started to quaver, and his whole body was trembling.

Peter took pity on him and fetched him a glass of water.

'Thanks,' Napier took a deep breath as if he was approaching the end of a race. 'The letter made me sick.' He hesitated, unable to finish the horror. 'He told me that on the evening Laura died Lomax and Team had been playing around with cocaine, and he, that bastard Team had practically forced the stuff into Laura's arm. Minutes later she was unconscious.'

Napier's voice was breaking up, and he tried not to sob.

'That all happened in the lane just outside the Master's house, so they carried her in to get help.'

He stopped to wipe the tears from his eyes and to marshal his words.

'At first I couldn't understand why students would go for help to the Head of the College, but apparently Lomax in his student days was queer. Maybe he still is. Anyway he and my uncle had been having it off, and so Lomax had my uncle by the balls in more ways than one. My uncle knew that if Lomax spilled the beans to the university authorities he would lose the Mastership. So he agreed to help those bastards, he had to, he was being blackmailed. So they set the whole thing up. They took Laura to the river in the back of my uncle's car, took her to the jetty, jammed some wood splinters into her arm to cover up the injection and—and—'

He choked with grief, while Peter sat transfixed, waiting for the old man to steady himself.

'And?'

'They dropped her in like a sack of rubbish.'

'Pigs,' spat Peter. He had expected to hear about corruption, but nothing like this. After a long silence Napier continued.

'The cover-up was easy,' he said. There was a hard edge to his voice. '*Too* bloody easy. My uncle was a pathologist, he was in charge of all the autopsies at that hospital.'

'Addenbrookes,' said Peter.

'Yes, that's it. Addenbrookes. No one would doubt the word of a Professor of Pathology, so that was it. Fake evidence, and so the inquest said it was an accidental death.'

Another long silence. There was a lot to take in. The flow of information had been totally overwhelming, forcing both men into contemplation, with Napier grieving and Peter thinking. He was desperately trying to make a connection with Ciencia, then suddenly it came.

'What's your daughter's name?' he asked.

'Antonia,' said Napier. He was puzzled. 'Why do you ask?'

Another bull's-eye; it couldn't be coincidence. The directors of Ciencia were Juan and Antonia Lopez.

'So how does she like running Ciencia?' probed Peter.

'She seems to like it,' answered Napier automatically. He stopped short. 'Oh, you know about that.'

'I didn't till now,' replied Peter. 'I need to know it *all*.' His voice was hard. 'And I mean *all*, every bit. No lies, no fudges.' He tapped the truncheon on Napier's knee again.

Again his victim was unfazed. 'You don't need to threaten me,' he said calmly.' I said I'd tell you it all, and I will. I'm sure Antonia wasn't involved in any murder. Anyway, who was murdered? You said it was a friend.'

'She was a technician working on the cytocide testing. On Wednesday she discovered some fiddle or irregularity that was going on at Clerkenwell. Four days later she was killed by a car that was deliberately driven at her.'

Napier seemed genuinely stunned. 'I'm sorry. Really sorry. I didn't want anyone hurt like that. I didn't want anyone hurt at all. Just those swine. Lomax and Team.'

'So how were you going to do that? All you've got is a statement from a dying man about something which happened forty years ago. No proof at all.'

Napier grinned triumphantly. 'But I do. I didn't tell you all of it. When my uncle agreed to help out he insisted that they all take collective responsibility for what they were doing. He typed up three copies of a statement of what they'd all done, and all three signed each copy and kept one each. A sort of mutual insurance. My uncle sent his copy to me in his letter. My solicitors have got it for safekeeping, just in case anything happened to me.'

'So why didn't you expose them? And how the hell does testing come in to all of this?'

Napier paused, getting his thoughts in order. 'I almost did expose them, but then I changed my mind. It was Antonia I was thinking of. She and Juan at Ciencia had put a huge amount of money into cytocide and yet the results were very variable. When I found out that Lomax was the director of MICR I thought we were in with a chance. Do the testing there, and if MICR says cytocide works like a charm we're on to a winner. Ciencia would sell the patent to Thirsk and cover all its debts. So we told Lomax what we wanted, and what I would do if he didn't comply. All he and Team had to do was produce results showing that cytocide worked.'

Peter understood at last, but there was still one piece of the jigsaw not in place.

'One thing doesn't make sense,' he said. 'Two technicians were talking at Clerkenwell about the testing. No one else was there, and Susan, the one who is in hospital, says they definitely didn't tell anyone else about what they'd seen. So how did killer know what they'd discovered?'

Napier looked guilty. 'I forgot that,' he said. 'Ciencia bought the building in Clerkenwell and fitted it with microphones so that they could monitor what was going on. They record everything in the flat at the back. Lomax told Thirsk he was on the lookout for animal facilities and suggested Clerkenwell as it was ideal. So Ciencia have been calling the shots from day one. They obviously heard your friends' conversation and decided to do something about it before it became public news.' He stopped, overcome with emotion. 'I'm so sorry, I knew Juan was ambitious, and that he could be ruthless, but I didn't expect this.'

He slumped back in the chair, totally exhausted, and for a moment Peter thought he was going to have another angina attack.

'You look dreadful,' he said gently. 'You should be in bed.' He lifted Napier out of the chair and walked him into the bedroom. 'Get in. I'll get you a drink.'

Back in the kitchen Peter made Napier another cup of tea and took it to the old man.

'I'm off now, and thank you for all your help. I'm sorry I threatened you.'

Napier nodded, and turned his head into the pillow.

Peter stayed on until he was absolutely sure that Napier was alright. He sat in the sitting room irritably going through the questions he should have asked, and reviewing what he had been told. After half an hour he went back into the bedroom, where Napier was snoring peacefully. He smiled, tucked the bedclothes around the old man's neck and went back into the sitting room. He picked up his truncheon and left.

On the A30 he stopped at a phone box in a lay by and phoned the Institute.

'This is Dr Stott,' he said. 'Could you tell me if Dr Lomax and Dr Team are in today?'

'The Director is definitely not in,' she said. 'I'm not sure about Dr Team. I'll put you through to his secretary.'

Team's secretary confirmed that her boss was in. 'Shall I tell him that you want to see him?'

'No thanks. It's a surprise.'

It's going to be the biggest surprise that bastard ever had, thought Peter furiously. He was gripping the steering wheel so hard that his hands hurt, and he floored the accelerator, keeping a tight lookout in his rear mirror. The MG sped along to London, escaping the eyes of the police, and Peter had it parked in Lincoln's Inn Fields just after two that afternoon. Still in his hiking clothes, and with the truncheon in his rucksack he ran up the Institute stairs to Team's office. The secretary opened her mouth to say 'hello', saw his face, and said nothing. He barged straight past her into the office where her boss was sitting in his usual chair.

'Hello Peter,' he said. 'How are things? How's Susan?'

Peter's control snapped. He wrenched the truncheon from his rucksack, and, using it like a hammer, swung it into Team's chest. His colleague doubled up with a groan, and Peter locked the door.

'Now listen, you bastard,' he hissed. 'I know it all, every damn thing. Laura Marshall, cocaine, Lomax, Ciencia, testing. The lot. And the Ilford killing. And you have the gall to say "how's Susan". Just give me one good reason why I don't beat the pulp out of you before I turn you in.'

Team hauled himself up, clutching his chest.

'Christ, it hurts. I think my ribs are cracked.'

'Tough. That's not too much punishment for a double murderer.'

'If you're talking about Susan's mother I swear I knew nothing about it.'

Team's white face beamed back his innocence.

'So you're just a single murderer. What about Laura Marshall? Napier said you jammed cocaine in her arm.'

Team took his time answering. 'I know I've done some bad things in my time, but I didn't force Laura to take cocaine. She came to me, she knew I used it and she wanted to try it out. It was her last night in Cambridge, she wanted to celebrate and get high. She injected herself and we found her unconscious later.'

'Then you three bastard academics dropped her in the river.'

Team's face was like a mask. 'Yes, and I've been living with the consequences for the last forty years.'

With a huge effort Peter managed not to smash his truncheon over Team's head.

'You really are the most selfish pig I've ever met. So *you've* been living with it, poor bloody you. What about Napier?'

The two men eyed each other, and Peter changed direction.

'This is it,' he said. 'You know that.'

Team nodded.

'Yes,' he said. 'In my heart I'm glad. I didn't want any of this testing. I wanted to tell Ciencia to go to hell and take the consequences. But my department was being cut back, I'm sure Lomax was making sure I didn't get any contracts. So I went along with it.'

Peter didn't want to hear any more pathetic excuses.

95

'So fill me in on the details. What about cytocide? You were so damned sure it didn't work that you didn't even inject the animals with it.'

Team's face became slightly animated. 'That's where you're wrong. It *does* work, or to be exact Deidre's purified stuff does. The unpurified cytocide doesn't. It showed a small effect with the He-La cells, and the initial results with the rats were poor. Then I hooked into Deidre's experiment showing two types of cytocide and I used her method to separate the two. I tried out fraction one on Janet, and she's still here, still in reasonable health. All the cytocide supplied by Ciencia was purified and used to keep her alive. Massive amounts. She should have been dead months ago. I'm glad I did it, I've really got no conscience about it.'

There was a long silence.

'This really is the end,' said Peter. 'You know that, Ron,'

Team nodded.

'I'll give you till tomorrow morning,' said Peter. 'Then I go to the police. It's up to *you* what you do between now and then.' He looked hard at Team. 'But not Janet.'

Team nodded. 'No, not Janet.'

Peter nodded back, and slammed out past Team's cringing secretary.

In the park opposite he bought a cup of tea from the kiosk and sat behind a tree, watching. He didn't have long to wait. Within twenty minutes Team came down the steps of the Institute and walked ashen faced towards Holborn Station. Peter was pleased to see that he was still clutching his ribs. Danger gone, Peter went back into the Institute, where he telephoned the hospital, who told him that Susan was doing well, but was still sedated. He could come and see her if he wanted.

There was a nurse and a policeman in the ward when Peter got there. Susan looked much the same, but Peter was relieved to see that the infusion line in her arm had gone. Her bruised face was virtually unchanged, and she was tossing restlessly, muttering to herself. The policeman, who was trying to make out what she was saying, looked up when he saw Peter.

'Dr Stott, it's you. She keeps mentioning your name, says there's something important she needs to tell you, and that she mustn't tell anyone else.'

'She told me it last time I was here,' said Peter.' She's obviously forgotten.'

'And what was it, sir? Is it relevant to the case?'

'It was just some important results they'd got,' said Peter, lying easily.

'You're quite sure of that?' The policeman looked hard at him, and Peter was tempted to tell the truth. Then he remembered his agreement with Team, and continued lying. 'Quite sure. It was just about the level of drugs they were administering in their experiment.'

'If you say so, sir.' With that the policeman went back to his chair in the hall, leaving Peter with his assistant. He took her hand and spoke to her, but she didn't respond, and he looked carefully at her face, realising that the stitching had been done with great skill and that with luck the scars shouldn't be too bad. That cheered him up, and he stayed with her for another half hour while she slept on. He studiously ignored the policeman when he left, and walked to the post office down the street where he sent a telegram to Anne.

'Please call tomorrow afternoon. Missing you. Love Peter.'

The drive back to Maidenhead was awful. It was rush hour, the A4 was jammed, and it was drizzling steadily. Peter forced himself into staying awake by turning the car radio up full blast, and after surviving a near miss he got himself home safely. Indoors he kicked off his boots and crawled into bed. He was asleep in minutes.

The nap refreshed him and he awoke ravenously hungry and went downstairs to look hopefully into the fridge. Nothing, just sterilized milk. No bread in the bin; hell, he'd forgotten to buy some. He found a tin of baked beans in the cupboard, but the prospect of eating them without toast did not appeal. He knew he needed a good meal, so he rang around to find a restaurant that served suppers till late. It was in Henley, some distance away, but Peter enjoyed the drive. The meal was excellent, the wine was good and Peter was able to relax a little. It would all be over if Team had done the honourable thing, and if he hadn't the next step was the police tomorrow.

On the drive back he carefully thought out the slightly potted version of events that he would tell Inspector Grey next morning, and he was so busy with his thoughts that he didn't notice a car being parked a few yards from his gate. Inside the house he threw off his clothes and fell into bed.

It was Peter's full bladder that saved his life that night. After an hour's sleep he got up to go to the toilet, and from the landing he heard the tinkle of glass from the scullery. His heart raced and he went to the study to dial 999.

'This is emergency services. What service do you require?'

'Police, urgently,' he whispered. 'At 22, River Road, in Maidenhead. I have a burglar on the premises. Hurry please.'

Peter put the receiver down on the floor, and from the mantelpiece picked up the large solid silver elephant which had occupied pride of place in his father's shop. He eased the door open, and slid out onto the landing, where he could see the beam of a torch moving around the hall. His heart was in his mouth and his hands were sweating, but he forced himself to concentrate. He knew that the fifth stair creaked and that it would be his signal for action. When it came he switched on the hall light. The man on the stairs swung round to look at the lightened room below, and Peter saw his swarthy profile. It was the man from Clerkenwell who had dislocated his shoulder. Peter gasped, and the man swung the torch beam upwards to see the source of the noise. The last thing he saw in life was the flash of light on metal as Peter hurled the silver elephant down upon his head.

The man's body slid down the stairs into the pool of light at the bottom and Peter could see the twisted neck and the blood trickling out of the left ear. The position of the body reminded him of the Mau Mau terrorist he'd killed in Kenya. He had been shaking then, and he was shaking now, and in his study his fingers were trembling so badly that he could hardly pour whisky into his glass. From the landing he could see what looked like a tin can on the stairs, and then he realised it was a pistol fitted with a large home-made silencer. It had been a damned close thing. He didn't go near the body, he just sat on the landing, shaking and drinking, and he was still shaking when the police arrived.

Chapter 8
Truth and Consequences

Anne was in the kitchen when she saw the telegraph boy walking down the path. Her mother anxiously answered the front door and brought the envelope into her daughter.

It must be from Peter,' she said. 'I hope he's all right.'

Anne tore open the envelope, and scanned the text.

'He's missing me,' she said, handing over the telegram.

'Ah,' replied Mum. 'Isn't he sweet?'

The telegram asked Anne to call in the afternoon, and she assumed Peter would be at work. At three o'clock she put Michael in his pram, walked the half mile to the post box, and phoned the lab. A young male voice answered.

'Sorry Mrs Stott, Dr Stott isn't here. We haven't seen him since he went on holiday.'

'You've not seen him? But he went home on Sunday.' Anne's voice rose and her heart was racing. 'Where's Susan? Doesn't she know where he is?'

'Susan is in hospital, Mrs Stott. She was in a bad car accident. She has broken her leg and her face was badly cut. Her mother was killed.'

'Dear God.'

Anne just stood there, trying to speak, and the money ran out. She fished some coins out of her purse and phoned home. She let it ring and ring, but there was no answer.

Back home Mum tried to put a brave face on things.

'There must be a simple explanation for this,' she said, but she was as worried as Anne. Just after six they went back to the phone box, pushing Michael in his pram, but no one answered in Maidenhead. Both women were distraught. Mum was for calling the police immediately, but Anne was less sure.

'I'll give it one last try,' she said slowly. 'I'll ring again about nine. If there is no answer then it'll have to be the police.'

They killed time for the next few hours by listening to the radio, while not actually taking in anything that came over the airwaves. Finally Anne picked up her torch, put on her coat and walked out into the drizzle. From the upstairs bedroom Mum watched her as the torch picked its lonely way through the puddles and the trees. When Anne finally saw the glow of the kiosk in the distance she hesitated, almost unable to do what she knew she had to. In her mind she was almost certain that Peter wouldn't answer, and she didn't want to face that reality. Finally she forced herself to put the coins into the box and dialled home. She counted the rings, and when she got to ten she almost gave up. Then, to her delight, a tired voice cut in.

'Hello.'

She pressed button A.

'Peter, is that you?' Her relief was turning to fury. 'Where the hell have you been?'

'Anne, darling.' His voice broke. 'It's so lovely to hear your voice.'

The sob in his voice turned her anger into concern. 'Peter, what on earth have you been doing? We were worried sick, Mum and I. Are you alright?'

'As right as anyone can be who spent the last seventeen hours in Maidenhead police station,' said Peter. He sounded almost laconic. 'We had a burglar in the house last night, I caught him coming in and I killed him. It was him or me, he had a gun.'

There was a long, long silence.

'Anne, are you still there?'

'Yes, I'm still here, I'm trying to take all this in. Dear God, did he hurt you? What was he after?' She pushed some more coins in the slot. 'Are you alright?'

'Yes, I'm fine. I wasn't hurt. It was self-defence, but the police have to do their job. I am okay, really. But do come home, *please*. What's the number in your box?'

She told him, and when her money rang out he called her back. He didn't tell her the whole story, just about the burglary and his treatment by the police, and at the end she was in tears from relief and anxiety.

'We'll take the sleeper down tomorrow night. Look after yourself, darling. I'll phone you from Paddington. God, I can't go a whole day without talking to you. I'll call you tomorrow when we get to Oban.'

'That would be lovely. Look after yourselves. All love. Bye.'

Peter put the phone down, and crawled back into bed. Sleep was impossible. He saw it all, the blood on the stairs, him picking his way past the body to let the police in, them calling for reinforcements for the major incident, and the interminable interrogation at the police station.

'You say you know this man?'

'I know him because he dislocated my arm. I don't know who he is.'

'And I suppose you don't know why he apparently came to kill you?'

'Yes, I think I do.'

'Then would you care to enlighten us, sir?' The questioner, a previously pleasant detective called Johnson, was becoming sarcastic. 'Strangely enough we don't get many burglars with murder in mind.'

'Look,' said Peter. 'It's all involved with the killing of a technician of mine in Ilford. It has to be. The man in charge up there is Inspector Grey. You need to speak to him and tell him what's happened. If you get him down here, I'll go through it all with you from beginning to end. It will save time. He's the only one I'll talk to.'

Despite their objections Peter had stuck resolutely to his guns. The inspector was awakened in the middle of the night and drove irritably to Maidenhead. Fortified with two black coffees, and accompanied by Johnson, he angrily confronted Peter.

'This had better be good, Dr Stott,' he snapped. 'I know you have knowledge of these killings. All I want is the truth. I think that, up till now, you have been economical with it. So let's hear it all, fact by fact. If not, we'll throw the book at you.'

So Peter told his story, from his suspicions about the contracts to the confrontation with Team. He was objectively truthful in almost everything, but he didn't mention threatening Napier with the truncheon. The inspector listened to it all with a mixture of admiration, disbelief and fury, and fury finally prevailed.

'What the hell did you think you were doing?' he exploded. 'Playing devil's advocate? Why in God's name didn't you tell us everything you got from Napier? Why the hell did you go to confront Team? All you did was very nearly get yourself killed and give those bastards a head start.'

Peter was appropriately contrite. 'I'm sorry. I felt betrayed by Ron Team. He used to be a friend. I just wanted to beat the hell out of him.'

'And did you?'

'I thumped him in the chest with the truncheon,' said Peter with satisfaction. 'When you find him you'll find that his ribs are badly bruised.'

'That's the point. We don't have him.' The inspector was still seething. 'Why didn't you turn him into us?'

'I gave him time to sort himself out,' said Peter, telling a white lie. 'I told him he had till this morning; then I would go to the police. It was a big mistake.'

'An incredibly stupid one for a man of your intelligence,' snapped Johnson. 'I can hardly believe you did it. You were blocking our progress, just as you were when you didn't tell us about Napier in Hampshire. By the way, where do Team and Lomax live?'

'Ron and his wife live in Bromley in Kent,' said Peter. 'I don't know the address, I've never been there. Lomax has a flat in Greenwich, I've been there. I think it's 52, London Road.'

The inspector jotted down the information. 'I've got to contact Scotland Yard and the Kent police. Then I'll come back, we'll go through it all again and eventually we'll get your statement typed up.'

Peter sat nervously as he waited, and when Grey returned the interrogation continued with a vengeance. The probing was relentless, trying to find a flaw in Peter's story, but he held his own.

'So you've no idea who your burglar was?'

'No.'

'You just saw him at the factory?'

'Yes.'

'And he dislocated your arm? A nasty assault. And you didn't report it to the police?'

'I didn't want to wise up Lomax and Team.'

'And when he came up the stairs, did you yell out or warn him?'

'No.'

'So you just slammed the elephant down on his head?'

'Yes.'

And so it went on, seemingly for ever. It was just past seven when they finally typed up his statement and he signed it.

'Can I go home now?' he asked.

'I am afraid not,' said Grey. 'Your house is still a crime scene. Forensics are still there. I think you should stay here. We'll get you some breakfast and then you can get some rest.'

The exhausted Peter was allowed to sleep for almost four hours in a cell, before he was awakened by a friendly sergeant.

'Sorry sir, Inspector Grey would like to see you in about ten minutes in the interview room. We have some new information.'

Peter felt a new sense of apprehension which was not helped by Grey's icy manner.

'You seem to be attracting violence, Dr Stott. The body count is now approaching that of a Shakespearean tragedy. Now we have three more deaths.'

'Dear God.' Peter was shocked. He was expecting only one. 'So who's dead?'

'The Teams. The Kent police went to their house and got no answer. They had to break in. They found Mrs Team's body in the bedroom, and her husband's in the hall. It looks like murder followed by suicide.'

Peter went pale. That bastard Team, he'd promised not to hurt his wife.

'Unusual weapon,' mused Grey. 'A 9 mm Berretta automatic. Don't see them very often.'

A cold hand crawled down Peter's spine. With a huge effort he continued the conversation.

'So who else is dead?'

'Have a guess.'

'Lomax?'

'Got it in one.'

'How?'

'He was murdered. Shot in the head.'

Peter just sat there, taking it all in, trying not to be sick. It was almost a minute before he spoke.

'I don't believe this. When I spoke to Team at the Institute I said I'd give him till the next morning. Time to do the honourable thing, so to speak. And he assured me he wouldn't hurt his wife. Something's wrong. Really wrong. Ron hates—hated guns, he wouldn't join the gun club at the Institute. If he was going to kill himself he'd have taken the necessary drug. After all, he was an expert. And where would he get an automatic at such short notice?'

Grey stared at the table for another full minute before replying, and when he looked up his face was ashen. 'It's early days,' he said carefully. 'We need to know if the same gun killed Lomax and the Teams. If so, it would appear that Ron Team killed Lomax in revenge and then shot his wife and himself. It would have been easy enough, after all, it's only about half an hour's drive between the houses. But if what you say is correct it puts a completely different slant on things. It means that last night two killers were on the loose, one dealing with you and the other in London. Until we are sure about this, you and Susan are in extreme danger. We'll give you a police guard at home until we're sure of things. And we can't be sure of anything until the bodies have been autopsied. Anything else you want to tell me?'

'No,' replied Peter. 'That's it, everything.'

'Right,' said Grey. 'Now, we need a new final statement from you. It must be totally accurate, warts and all. When the case comes to trial you will certainly be called as a witness, and you'll be crucified if your statement doesn't stand up to scrutiny. So let's get on with it.'

So they did it all again, in agonising detail at an agonisingly slow pace. Hours later they read his statement back to him and Peter signed it. By this time, Grey was looking less irritable and Peter risked a question.

'Any news on my burglar?'

'Nothing really. He had no identification on him, and the car was stolen in east London two days ago. Needless to say we are checking his fingerprints. But we do have some progress elsewhere. We asked the Hampshire police to check up on the Lopezes. No one at home. So we suspect the husband. He's got the most to lose. He's Spanish, so he may try to get to his homeland. After all, there's no extradition treaty between Spain and Britain. So, if he gets there, he's safe. But we've notified

Interpol and the ports. By the way, this has become a major crime investigation, and as one of the killings took place in London, Scotland Yard have taken over. I expect they will need to talk to you. So expect a trip to up there.'

The exhausted Peter finally got home at six that evening, delivered to his gate by an unmarked police car. The phone was ringing as he opened the door, but he couldn't answer it in time. He picked his way up the blood soaked stair carpet and went to bed, sleeping the sleep of the dead until the phone rang again. He got there just in time.

'Anne darling, it's you.' He was overjoyed. 'It's so lovely to hear your voice.'

They talked for a long time, and hours later Peter was wide awake, still going through the horrors of the past day. He went into the study for more whisky, and as he looked cautiously out of the window he saw the comforting glow of a cigarette in the police car outside. Thank God for that; he felt safe at last, and he put on his favourite record. The exquisite piano chords of Beethoven's Emperor concerto hung like jewels in the dark, and Peter's eyes began to fill. He sobbed with relief at being alive, and choked with guilt over what he'd done to Susan and her mother. The spasms racked him again and again until he was drained, and he fell asleep in his study chair.

An aching back and raging hunger drove Peter downstairs next morning. After he'd gingerly picked his way past the blood on the stairs, he found fresh milk on the doorstep, so he made some tea and took it to the car outside. The young policeman nodded gratefully.

'I'd give you something to eat,' said Peter. 'But there's nothing in the house. I need to do some shopping.'

'I'll check it out for you, Mr Stott.' He switched on his radio and spoke to his boss. 'That's fine, but I've got to go with you. So you'll have a free taxi ride with me. Want to go now?'

'Please,' said Peter. 'I want to be home when my wife calls.'

The phone rang just after ten as Peter and his policeman had finished their eggs and bacon. Peter knew it would be Anne; the Oban ferry arrived from Mull just before the hour.

'Peter, are you really all right?' She sounded almost hysterical with worry.

'I'm fine, and I was safe. I am sitting here in our kitchen, eating breakfast under the protection of a nice policeman. It's so lovely to hear you, darling. How's Michael?'

'He's asleep. Mum's here with him. She came on the ferry with me for company. She's sick with worry.'

'Tell her not to be, and give her my love and thanks for everything. I'll see you tomorrow. If for some reason I can't make it to King's Cross, for goodness sake take a taxi to Paddington. Don't struggle on the underground with Michael.'

'I'll do that,' she said. 'So what's happening today?'

'That depends on the police,' said Peter. 'But I've got to do some cleaning. Look after yourself. I can't wait to see you both.'

'Me too,' she said. 'Bye darling.'

Cleaning was more easily said than done. The stair carpet covering the bottom six steps was a mass of congealed blood. Peter unscrewed the rods holding the bloodied section of the carpet in place, and carried the stained brass into the garden where he hosed it off. Using Anne's best kitchen knife he cut the carpet above the bloodstain, rolled it up and, with a shudder, put it in the dustbin. Then he scrubbed the woodwork furiously with soap and bleach until the natural pine shone through. Finally, he swept up the broken glass in the scullery and nailed some wood across the broken pane. He still had filthy hands when Deirdre Pearce rang.

'Peter, where on earth have you been? We expected you back Monday morning. Susan's—'

'I know about Susan,' he interrupted. 'I've been dealing with it. That's what I've been doing since Sunday, and I'm still dealing with it.'

'Dealing with it?'

'Deirdre, just trust me. I can't say anything. But I need to ask you a big favour.'

'Of course. Just ask.'

'Could you keep an eye on my department for a day or two? I'll tell them to report to you if there is a problem, or they can get me at home. I may be away until the weekend.'

'Peter, what the hell is going on? Should Lomax know about this?'

Peter laughed inwardly. 'He doesn't need to know anything. I can't say what's going on. But be warned. It's all about to go really pear shaped. Thanks, Deirdre, I owe you one.'

He rang off before she could answer.

Next he rang the lab and told the most senior technician what had been decided. The young man tried to find out what was going on, but Peter slapped him down.

'You work for me. This is a difficult time and I would value your help, not your questions. You'll know in good time.'

Just as Peter put the phone down, it rang again. This time it was Detective Johnson.

'Hello, Dr Stott. I'm sorry to bother you, but Scotland Yard insist on talking to you. Your minder will drive you in and we'll arrange transport.' He stopped. 'Don't worry, there's no problem.'

At the station Johnson was upbeat.

'We intercepted the Lopez pair at Dover, and arrested them on the charges of corruption and conspiracy to commit murder. That's just to hold while the Yard interrogates them and Napier. Our Senor Lopez wasn't armed when they arrested him.'

Peter was elated.

'That's marvellous news. But what do Scotland Yard want now?'

'They just want to go through your statement with you and bone up on the details before they grill anybody. And they specifically asked that you mention nothing of this when you're at work. The Lomax-Team deaths haven't been announced yet. The driver is ready to go if you are.'

'Okay,' said Peter. This nightmare seemed endless. 'Let's get it over with, once and for all. After that can I go to the hospital?'

'I imagine so. I am sure we could give you half an hour.'

'Oh,' remembered Peter, 'what about my burglar?'

'No news yet. But he must be connected to the Lopez duo in some way. If not, why would they be doing a runner?'

The drive to London was tolerable, as was the interview with Scotland Yard. Peter made a point of being frank, informative and completely honest, and they obviously believed everything he said. All they wanted was amplification of some important points, and Peter basked in their unspoken admiration at what he and Susan had done.

After that it was the hospital. Peter's driver sat down next to the policeman in the corridor while Peter walked into the ward. His assistant was not alone; she was talking to a middle-aged woman whom she introduced as Aunt Alice. Susan looked marginally better, the puffiness in her face had reduced and she had brushed her hair forward to cover the stitches on her right cheek. She managed a delighted, if painful smile.

'Aunt Alice says she's going to help out at home when I get out,' she said. 'But they say it'll be weeks before I'm out of this plaster cast, and I don't want Mum buried—' her eyes filled 'until I can be at the funeral.'

'That's all organised,' said Alice soothingly. 'So don't worry about it. Just get better, and we'll have it then.'

Susan wiped the tears from her eyes and switched subjects.

'Peter,' she said. She was still distressed. 'The police keep saying that Mum and I could have been deliberately run down. Why would anyone do that?'

Peter was brutally honest. 'I'm afraid it was done to keep you quiet,' he said. 'The police are right, it was murder.'

The two women clutched each other and wailed at the certain knowledge that their respective sister and mother had been executed.

'But why?' sobbed Susan again.

'Are you ready for it all?' asked Peter. 'It's got much worse.'

They nodded, and so he told them. By now he was getting good at it. When he'd just finished his police driver came in to collect him, and so he had to leave the two women in tears and in total shock. Back in Maidenhead they told him that he still had police protection overnight, but as the chief suspects were in custody it would be withdrawn next morning unless circumstances changed.

Almost all the workers at the Institute travelled into central London by train. Some read the Daily Telegraph, and if so they would have seen a small article on page five saying that Dr Lomax, the head of the Marshall Institute for Cancer Research, had been found shot dead at his home. The police were regarding his death as suspicious. Readers of the News Chronicle would also have found a similar article about the deaths of Ron Team and his wife. So chaos reigned when everyone arrived at work. Secretaries were in tears, and scientists drifted from lab to lab gossiping and trying desperately to make sense of it all. Paul Stephens, the deputy director cancelled his surgery at the Marsden Hospital and came straight round to the Institute. His first act was to telephone or telegraph the Heads of the Departments to say there would be an emergency meeting next morning at ten.

Peter got his telegram when he arrived home at Maidenhead with Anne and Michael. He immediately rang Deirdre Pearce to say that he'd be there at the meeting and to make sure things were going well. She tried to find out what was going on, but Peter put her off.

'I'll tell you it all tomorrow Deirdre. I promise. I'll tell all the Heads at the same time. Then I don't have to keep going over it.'

He had been over it in detail with Anne on their trip back from London. When they had met at King's Cross she had collapsed with relief at seeing him, and they'd clung to each other, both in tears. He'd told her the full story, warts and all, on the Maidenhead train, sitting alone in a first-class compartment. Anne listened to it all with amazement and anger mixed with relief.

'I was so worried about you. You were so preoccupied. At first I thought you were having an affair, then I changed my mind. But I knew something was wrong and that you were keeping something from me.'

'I know,' said Peter. 'I shouldn't have done it. At the beginning I just thought you'd think I was becoming paranoid— so I didn't tell you any of it. Then it became habit. I shouldn't have done it.'

'No, you shouldn't have,' she said, her relief suppressing her anger. 'I'll forgive you this time; just don't do it again. No more secrets.'

'Absolutely,' agreed Peter. 'No more secrets. Ever.' He kissed her to make the pact complete.

For the rest of the day, Peter felt reasonably happy but Anne was uneasy in their house of death. He went in to town, had some glass cut and fitted it into the broken window. All was now virtually normal, apart from the absence of part of the stair carpet and the overall smell of bleach, but Anne put her anxiety aside and cooked a fantastic supper and they had an early night.

By the next day, the newspapers had got their act together and all of them had linked the Lomax-Team deaths under headlines such as "Murders at Top Science Centre". The News Chronicle had even linked in the earlier death of Denise Preston, and so the Institute was alive with rumours and theories. When he arrived there, Peter took a phone call and then went directly to the meeting of the Heads. The other three looked sick and worried, but Peter radiated confidence. After all, he knew everything.

Stephens opened the proceedings.

'As you know, in a completely unprecedented event, we have lost two of our most valuable colleagues in the most tragic circumstances,' he said in his usual patrician way. 'Peter, Deidre says that you may know something of what's been happening. Could you please update us as to what you know.'

So Peter went through it all yet again, and his ten minute account was followed by an hour of stunned discussion. Finally the exhausted Stephens called the meeting to a temporary close.

'I suggest we have an early lunch,' he said. 'We'll resume just after one, and get down to the nitty-gritty as to how we proceed from here.'

The actual nitty-gritty involved a temporary but wholesale restructuring of the Institute. Two of Deidre's assistants from biochemistry who specialised in cell structure were moved to Paul Ince's histology department. Team's pharmacology department was divided unequally, with two thirds of the staff joining Deirdre Pearce in biochemistry. The other third went to Peter's oncology, and he was put in charge of all the animal facilities. Stephens, the new acting director, said he would reduce his surgery down to one day a week so that he could concentrate on running the Institute. All this was agreed, and the director's secretary typed up a copy of the agreement which all the Heads signed. By half past three it was done, and Peter walked out onto the elegant steps at the front of the Institute and sat down in the warm October sun. He felt triumphant; his efforts had been rewarded. His staff had doubled, and his pay would increase almost a third when the governors of the Institute ratified the agreement. Then he remembered his assistant, and set off purposefully to St Thomas's to see how she was.

Susan disliked being in hospital, but she hated the idea of going home. She knew that when she did she would have to face the reality of burying her mother, having the wake, and then living alone. She had had a few close friends from her school days, but they had all married and left the area, and they only dropped in to see her when they happened to be in Ilford. She desperately hoped that Aunt Alice would move in with her when she was discharged from hospital. If not, she knew she would feel desperately alone. She wasn't lonely in the ward: she had colleagues dropping in to say hello, the nurses were friendly, and Peter had kept in contact. Unpleasant as it was, the hospital was actually a cocoon from reality, and that reality was much nastier than life in the hospital.

She managed a brilliant smile through almost normal lips when Peter arrived. He grinned back in return.

'You're looking better,' he observed.

'I feel that I'm improving,' she replied. 'The pain's almost gone, and they're going to try me out on crutches on Monday if the consultant says it's alright.'

'I'm impressed,' he said, and he was. 'Want to hear the news from the Institute?'

The news that excited her most was the fact that she would be promoted in Peter's newly expanded department when she got her HNC.

'Thank you so much, Peter,' she beamed. 'I just hope I've passed.'

'Aunt Alice saw the letter from Barking Tech at your house this morning,' he said. 'She rang me at the Institute to ask if it would be all right to open it. I said yes. So who's a clever girl then?'

Susan's eyes widened. 'So I passed?'

'Sure as hell did. Well done indeed, Miss Susan Preston.' He gave her a congratulatory kiss on the forehead while she shrieked with delight. When she calmed down his guilt returned.

'It's not much after what I've put you through.'

'But it wasn't your fault,' she said.

'Yes it was, it was my own stupid fault.'

'There's nothing to feel bad about,' she replied. 'I wanted to do it. We wanted to do it. I was as much a part of it as you.'

'But you weren't involved with Janet Team's death. If I'd gone straight to the police she would still be alive.'

'But not for long,' said Susan. 'According to Ron Team it was only the cytocide he gave her which was keeping her alive. With him gone, she'd have died from the cancer.'

Peter nodded doubtfully. 'I suppose so.' Then he remembered. 'That reminds me, we need to get a full-scale autopsy report on Janet's body. After all, what we've got here by accident is a full-scale test of cytocide in the human body. It'll show whether cytocide was working and if it may show other side-effects. It's too good to miss. It's a chance in a lifetime'

Peter broached the subject of the autopsy when he rang Maidenhead police station that evening. Detective Johnson was upbeat about everything.

'I don't see why you shouldn't get a detailed autopsy report,' he said. 'But that's up to the coroner, and they are a law unto themselves. I'll broach the subject to him if you like. He could order a second autopsy, a more detailed one, if he thinks it's important enough. By the way, some news on Napier.'

Peter stayed silent. He hadn't asked about the old man before because he thought that Napier might have disappeared or be dead from angina.

'Is he all right?' he asked cautiously.

'He's fine, pretty fit. The Lopezes wouldn't talk at first. They said they were just escaping to Spain because the company was going broke. But old man Napier is really going to put the screws on his daughter so that she'll turn Queen's evidence against her husband. And as for your would-be killer, his name is John Martin. He used to work for Ciencia in so-called security. Most important, ballistics did show that the same gun was used to kill Lomax and the Teams.'

'Wow,' said Peter. 'So it's practically sown up.'

'Yes, Dr Stott. I really think it is.'

Anne was amazed that the police had dealt with the case so quickly, and was ecstatic at the news of Peter's promotion.

'It's no more than you deserve,' she said firmly as she uncorked a bottle of claret that Peter's father had laid down some twenty years ago. 'Let's drink to Dad, and to Michael.'

'And to Mum,' added Peter.

'Yes,' she said. 'And to Mum.'

Peter changed the subject. 'So how's our son and heir?'

'A bit fretful. He's got a bit of nappy rash, so I'll have to change him more often and slap on some Vaseline. That reminds me, I'd better do him now.' She gulped down her wine and went upstairs, with Peter following. While she changed the nappy he looked at the easel in the corner of the nursery.

'Wow,' he said. 'That's bloody different.'

It was. The sketch was for a new painting of the River Thames, with the moon appearing through the spectral clouds. The trees were gaunt and windswept, and the human figures were cowed in the face of Nature. It was almost Whistler at his bleakest. Behind it, on a second easel, was the painting that Anne had completed just before Michael's birth. It was sunny, alive and vibrant, and Peter realised how much the violence of the last few days had affected his wife.

'I like this one better,' he said, pointing to the second easel.

'So do I.'

Their view was not shared by the public. The pictures from Anne's so called dark period would be selling for huge sums just a year after her death.

Chapter 9
Horrid Nature

Peter was lounging on the riverbank with a fishing rod in his hand. It was a hot July afternoon, and all the family were in the garden. Michael was gurgling in his playpen under the shade of the oak tree, Anne was sketching and Mum was dozing in a deckchair. Peter smiled to himself; it looked like a postcard for the perfect family in the ideal garden. His float dipped, he struck, and a minute later he had yet another small roach in his keep net. Suddenly, water swirled violently below the willow. He picked up his spinning rod, quickly tied a lure onto the line and cast it accurately just short of the roots of the tree. At the second cast, the pike rose to the temptation and Peter let it swallow the bait completely before striking. The rod bent and Peter could feel the weight of a sizeable fish on the end. He played it carefully and drew it to the bank. In went the gaff, and Peter hauled the fish on to the bank. Michael shrieked with delight and both Anne and Mum came to have a look. Peter thumped the fish behind its head with a priest and it stopped thrashing.

'That's a good meal,' said Anne excitedly. She liked baked pike.

'Weighs about ten pounds,' replied Peter. 'More than one meal.'

With that he opened up his gutting knife, slit the fish along its underbelly, pulled out the entrails and flung them into the river. He rinsed out the gut cavity with the garden hose and put the fish in the kitchen refrigerator. The ladies admired it again and agreed to have it for tomorrow's supper.

After his catch, Peter sat in the garden sipping whisky and playing with Michael while the two women prepared supper. It had been a good day; in fact, it had been a good year, a very good year. A week ago, Michael had had his first birthday and he looked very well on it. He was the ideal baby; he only cried when something was seriously wrong, he had his mother's looks, his father's brains and he was well advanced for his single year. He was already standing unaided and was unusually tall for his age. The district nurse was amazed at his progress.

'We've got a real highflyer here,' she said smiling. 'I expect he'll be Prime Minister by the time he's thirty.'

'Or an artist,' responded Anne hopefully. 'But I expect he'll copy his dad and become a scientist.'

'So are you going to have another one?'

'Oh yes,' replied Anne. 'We hope to. I don't want him to be an only child like me. But I thought we'd wait until he's two.'

'That's best,' said the nurse vaguely. 'Space them out a bit.'

There had been two major events in Peter's past year, and both had involved the Institute. Almost six months to the day after Lomax's death the governors of the Institute had ratified the temporary reorganisation which Stephens had instigated. They'd found that they didn't need a replacement for Ron Team; the Institute was functioning perfectly well without him, and so Peter's and Deirdre's temporarily expanded departments had become permanent. Stephens had been confirmed as Director, a very popular appointment, and his old Department of Medicine was now headed by a Mr Watkins, a young surgeon from the Marsden Hospital.

Peter's second major event had been the trial at the Old Bailey which had lasted two weeks. He had been an excellent witness for the prosecution and the Press had been agog at how two scientists had investigated an old crime. The Chronicle's headline had been 'Scientific Sleuths Solve Mystery', while the Daily Telegraph had confined itself to 'Cancer Experts Crack Case'. Peter's evidence had merely set the scene, and it had been the evidence of the wife and the police forensics team which had been the most damning. Antonia Lopez had done what her father Napier had hoped and had become a major prosecution witness against her husband, saying that he had been absent all night on the day of the murders, returning only in the early hours to pack up for their escape to Spain. The hairs found in Ron Team's hand, presumably there as a result of a struggle, were shown to be from Juan Lopez's scalp and the paint found on the tree outside the Team's house matched that on the wing of the Lopez car. The slow accumulation of forensic and circumstantial evidence had proved damning, and after an hour's deliberation the jury had found Lopez guilty of murdering the Teams and Lomax. His wife was in hospital, having barbiturates pumped from her stomach when the judge donned the black cap and sentenced the emotionless Spaniard to death. In the trial after her recovery Antonia received only a six months sentence for corruption, which meant that she was able to care for her father in his final months.

Peter had also been hugely successful in his dealings with Thirsk. Not surprisingly, the company which financed the cytocide testing had been outraged at the corruption in the Institute and had considered taking legal action; but Peter and Stephens had finally talked them round, and their trump card had been the autopsy report on Janet Team which clearly stated that her liver cancer was in remission and that there were no more secondaries. Almost all the other internal organs were normal, but she did have pancreatitis.

At the meeting with the directors of Thirsk Stephens had been both profusely apologetic and upbeat.

'We all know that Lomax and Team were charlatans,' he said. 'And the Institute has paid a heavy price for their crimes. But, inadvertently, some good has come out of it all. Cytocide has actually been tested on a person with cancer, something which would never normally happen. And the results were astonishing: the tumour on the liver had regressed and Janet was in pretty good health when she was killed. So cytocide seems to work, and it's certainly worth another try.'

'And who's going to pay for it?' snapped Thirsk's managing director.

'We will,' said Peter. 'We'll do it all again, with extras, for free. And that would include a massive increase in cell testing and all our latest research into the structure of cytocide. That's the least we can do under the circumstances. That's it in outline, but we can firm up the details with you at a later date if you agree. I hope in principle that's okay with you.'

The Thirsk directors knew it was a good offer. They nodded at each other, and Peter continued.

'As you know the official receivers are selling off all of Ciencia's assets, and you should be able to buy the patent on cytocide for very little. And you'd have the advantage of knowing that it almost certainly works.'

'But what about the pancreatitis mentioned in the autopsy?' asked another director.

'It could have been due to the cytocide,' replied Peter cautiously. 'But I think it's extremely unlikely. She almost certainly had pancreatitis all along and didn't know she'd got it. The calcification is a strong indication that her pancreatitis was chronic. The pain from it would have been similar to that from the tumour. What we almost certainly do know for sure is that the cytocide acted against the liver cancer, and that's what it's all about.'

The Thirsk directors had agreed with him, and as he'd expected they'd managed to buy the cytocide patent for a relatively trifling amount. The animal testing was then restarted in earnest under Peter's tight supervision, and a meeting reviewing their progress was held the day after he'd caught the pike. Susan was now running the animal facilities at Clerkenwell, and she'd come round to the Institute to discuss progress with Peter and McDonald. The strain of the past months showed in her face, but she managed a bright smile for Peter.

'How's Michael?' she asked.

Peter was both flattered and intrigued. Since Michael's birth Susan had shown an almost obsessive interest in his son, and her interest was not waning.

'He's still as bright as ever. His big thing yesterday was seeing me catch a pike. I've never seen him so excited. Incidentally, do you like pike? If you do, I'll bring you in some.'

'I don't know, Peter. I'll ring Aunt Alice and see what she says. She's the cook now. But thanks for the offer.'

'Right,' he said. 'Ah, here's McDonald. Now we can get down to what we're here for.'

Their discussion lasted well over two hours. Peter evaluated their testing program in detail, checking every point and making sure that everything was being done as it should. The early animal results were looking promising, and the cytocide had a proven effect against the He-La cells. After the meeting, McDonald returned to his animal empire on the fifth floor, and

Peter took Susan to lunch in the cafeteria. She was looking forward to it as she rarely saw Peter now that she was working over in Clerkenwell. He, in turn, still felt an enormous guilt over the death of her mother, and was trying desperately to limit the damage and to get her to return to her previous cheerful self. He realised that he'd made a mistake in putting her in charge at Clerkenwell; he'd done it because he trusted her and because it gave his newly promoted technician a chance to show her mettle. And she'd been excellent, but the responsibility and the isolation from the main Institute had kept her worried and depressed. Peter now knew that she would have been much happier if she'd continued working jointly with Deirdre and him.

'It's nice to have a chat,' he said cheerfully as they sat down to eat. 'So how are things at home? You and Aunt Alice getting along?'

'Oh, we're fine, we get on really well, and it's lovely to have her. But—' she hesitated. 'But she's—'

'Not Mum,' added Peter quietly.

Susan nodded, and her eyes moistened. In silence they started on their soup.

'I'm very pleased at what you've done at Clerkenwell,' said Peter after the first few spoonfuls. 'You've proved yourself. Just hang in there, finish it off, and I'll make sure you come back here to the Institute when it's finished. You'd like that wouldn't you?'

'Yes please,' said Susan. Peter was delighted to see the old sparkle in her eyes. 'That would be lovely.'

'And Susan, you're always asking about Michael. Why don't you come down to Maidenhead and see him some weekend? Bring Alice if you want.'

Susan was amazed at the offer. 'But won't Anne mind?'

'Not at all. It's her idea.'

Peter was speaking the exact truth. Anne had realised way back that Susan was a rival for Peter's affections, and she'd decided to adopt a Sicilian solution to the problem. *Keep your friends close and your enemies closer.* To that end she wanted to see Susan and Peter together on her territory.

Susan was almost cheerful as she took the train home that evening. She'd enjoyed her lunch with Peter and was looking forward to seeing Michael again, and the prospect of working back in biochemistry was the icing on the cake; but, as always, the memories of the past year resonated in her head. Her year had slowly improved from a very low base. She'd stayed in hospital for almost three weeks and buried her mother five days after leaving it. Practically all the Institute staff had turned out for the funeral and the church was jammed, in stark contrast to the burials of the Teams and Lomax which were poorly attended. Susan had surprised herself and her friends by staying icily calm even in the graveyard, where Aunt Alice had hugged her as they threw their ritual handfuls of earth onto the polished coffin. With that done they'd walked into the church hall where Susan had hobbled painfully between the guests on her crutches, acting the perfect host. It was only at home that she'd finally broken down. It was over, her beloved mother had gone and she felt truly alone, even with Aunt Alice in her bedroom upstairs. She also knew they'd have to start clearing out her mother's things, but that was another horror to come and so they'd put it off until tomorrow. Worn out from crying, she'd laid down in her temporary bed on the living room sofa and fallen into an exhausted sleep.

Susan slept straight through until Aunt Alice brought in breakfast on a tray. She helped Susan get dressed and then looked directly at her.

'Are you ready for this?'

Her niece nodded, and hobbled to the stairs. She discarded her crutches and eased herself painfully upwards on her bottom. At the top, Alice helped her up, manoeuvred her along the landing and finally sat her in the small armchair in her mother's bedroom. As Susan watched Alice emptied all the wardrobes and tipped the clothes onto the bed. They decided what they wanted to keep and what would go to Oxfam, and the discards were put in pillowcases, which Aunt Alice took down to the hall. Finally she emptied her sister's jewellery box onto the counterpane.

'You first,' said Susan.

'You're sure?' asked Alice

Susan nodded, and Alice selected an emerald brooch. 'That's all I want.'

'I just want these two,' said Susan. She picked up her mother's engagement ring and the pearl ring she'd bought in Clerkenwell.

'Why the pearl?' Aunt Alice was being inquisitive.

'It's the last thing I gave her. Peter helped me buy it.'

119

'Did he indeed?'

Susan had the grace to blush.

'I'll get you downstairs,' said Alice, changing the subject. 'Then I'll get you settled and take the clothes to Oxfam. And the spare jewellery to Johnson's to see if they'll buy it. You'll be alright?'

'I'll be fine. But please ask Oxfam to send the clothes to another branch.' She hesitated, biting her lip. 'I don't want to see a stranger walking around in Mum's best dress.'

Her aunt hugged her, loaded the clothes into the A35 and drove off, leaving her niece to break down into tears as the car turned the corner. When she returned, Alice slowly moved her belongings into her sister's room, and Susan got her bedroom back. A new order was established.

Three weeks after Peter had mentioned it, both Aunt Alice and Susan were invited down to Maidenhead for Sunday lunch, and to Anne's surprise the day went remarkably well. She expected Susan to spend all her time chatting to Peter, but she was completely wrong. Her younger guest spent almost all her time playing with Michael, and that softened even Anne's suspicious heart. Against her better judgement, she started to see Susan's nicer characteristics, and even began to like her. She smiled at her son sitting on Susan's knee.

'Lady,' said Michael, poking Susan on her nose.

Peter laughed. 'That's Susan. Can you say Susan, Michael?'

'Soo-san,' gurgled his son, trying hard.

'*Auntie* Susan,' chipped in Anne, trying to be nice.

'*Lady* Susan,' said the determined Michael, having the last word.

They all laughed.

When they were leaving, Susan made a great point of thanking Anne.

'We both really loved it, Anne. Thank you so much for inviting us. Michael's so gorgeous.'

Anne responded with a peck on her cheek.

Aunt Alice had met Peter before at the hospital, but had never had a relaxed conversation with him. She had thoroughly enjoyed her day, and was impressed with everything at Maidenhead. Good food, good wine, nice weather and delightful company had made it a memorable day. On the drive back to Ilford she gushed enthusiastically to Susan.

'Peter really is a charmer,' she said. 'Intelligent and witty. I can see why you like him.'

Susan stayed silent.

'And Anne. She's charming too. So pretty, with those lovely eyes. And a figure to die for, despite the baby. And she paints so well—she showed me some of her pictures. I'd give my right arm for her looks and talent.'

'So would I,' said Susan bitterly. 'She's got *everything*.'

Alice looked hard at her niece and saw she'd struck a nerve. She changed the subject, and they talked about films and TV for the next ten minutes, but Susan was still edgy, and in desperation Alice changed the subject.

'So what have you got on at work tomorrow?' She really didn't want to know; she wasn't particularly interested in animal testing, but she did want to cheer Susan up. To her delight she got an enthusiastic response.

'We are starting the first big dissection on Tuesday, and we'll get an idea of whether the cytocide is working. I'm really looking forward to it after all this time. I can't *wait*.'

'So how will you know if it works?'

Susan gave a simplified answer. 'We use a lot of rats. All have been given a cancer-causing drug and half have been given a dose of cytocide. All we have to do is compare the size of the tumours in both groups. The group without cytocide is our reference, our control group.'

'Control is what I need for this damned car,' muttered Alice, changing the subject again and reverting to her favourite topic, the inadequacies of the A35. 'Steers like a truck.'

Susan laughed. 'Here we go. My favourite aunt's complaining again.'

Alice grinned and poked her niece in the ribs. They drove home happily together.

The next morning, the technicians were busy at Clerkenwell setting up the dissection room. They taped down waterproof paper onto the benches, fitted new blades to their scalpels, and filled sample bottles with formalin. Susan was ever present, checking on everything and making sure that everyone knew exactly what they were doing. The specifications for the overall testing of the cytocide were those prescribed by the Federal Drug Administration in the USA, and that meant that if the cytocide worked with no unwanted side effects it could be licensed for use in the largest pharmaceutical market in the world.

Just before nine o'clock the cages of rats were wheeled in on trolleys. All the animals had been starved overnight to empty their gut and make the dissection easier, but Susan knew it was going to be a hard slog. The dissection of one rat could take half an hour or more, particularly if a number of tumours were discovered, and forty rats were needed to check the efficacy of just one level of cytocide. The first group of ten had been injected with harmless saline, while the second group had all received saline containing the cytocide. Group 3 were animals which had been given the cancer-causing drug, butter yellow, for a month followed by daily injections of saline, while the animals in Group 4 had received the butter yellow followed by the 1 mg of cytocide dissolved in saline.

Susan put all the rats from Group 1 into a large glass tank fitted with a perforated floor below, which was a dish of chloroform. After a minute, the rats collapsed and were taken out. Their throats were cut with a scalpel and their blood collected for analysis. With the expertise of long experience, Susan slit the first rat from anus to throat and peeled back the skin. Using scissors she cut into the peritoneal cavity and exposed the abdominal organs. Each had to be individually dissected out, weighed and examined for abnormalities. Susan knew the list by heart—stomach, spleen, pancreas, small intestine, caecum, colon, and that was just for starters. The chest cavity which she exposed next contained the heart, lungs, oesophagus and trachea. And the brain was still to come.

With her team of four technicians, Susan completed the dissection on the Group 1 animals in about an hour. All were healthy with no tumours. The staff had a 10-minute tea break and then restarted on Group 3, the animals given butter yellow and no cytocide. As expected, the effect of this carcinogen was obvious: all the rats were thin and almost all had tumours, mainly in the liver. To Susan's delight, the results in the afternoon with Group 4 were equally obvious. Almost all the rats had tumours, but they were much smaller than in Group 3 and all the indications were that the cytocide really did have anti-cancer properties, but her delight faded slightly when her new technician David called her over to look at an organ.

'Susan,' he asked.' What do you make of that?'

'That' was the pancreas from a rat from Group 2. Instead of being white and soft it was grey and granular, with hard lumps in it. It also weighed less than usual

'I don't know,' replied Susan cautiously. But in her heart of hearts she did. In front of them were the classic signs of calcifying pancreatitis in an animal which had been exposed only to cytocide. 'Put it into the preserving fluid. I'll take it round to Ince's department myself.'

Susan, as usual, was correct. Later next day the histology department confirmed the pancreatitis, and it was not to be the only case. In later dissections where the rats had been exposed to the cytocide for a longer time the incidence of the pancreatitis increased, and it was also found in the animals with cancer which had been treated with the drug. The fact that the pancreatitis was appearing in about 10% of the healthy rats given cytocide was a potential death threat to the project, but on the positive side, the drug was showing a huge reduction in the size of the liver tumours.

Four months later, when all the results were collated, Director Stephens and Peter met with the Thirsk management to review the data and to decide how to proceed. As Stephen said, the ball was very much in Thirsk's court. They had a drug which had a huge proven record in suppressing cancer. On the other hand it would never get a licence until the problem of pancreatitis was resolved. If they could modify the cytocide to remove its anti-pancreatic properties Thirsk were onto a multibillion winner, but that research could be extremely costly. The Thirsk directors were totally divided, and agreed on a three week period of reflection before deciding the way forward after the Christmas holiday period. And it was over Christmas that the horror began in the Stott household.

Anne had suggested that Susan and her aunt come down to Maidenhead on the weekend before the festive period, and they were outside toddling around the garden with Michael when he fell down the step onto the patio and bruised his shin. He howled with pain, but after a lot of cuddling and motherly love he forgot all about it, and on Christmas Day, he was delighted with his new tricycle. Mum had come down from Scotland and was amazed to see how charming and advanced he was.

'Isn't he going to have a little brother or sister?' she asked Anne.

Her daughter blushed. 'What a question Mum. But yes, we hope to. We have been trying for another.'

Her mother smiled. 'That's marvellous news.'

Later that day, Michael bumped his shin on the pedal of the tricycle.

'Hurts, Mummy,' he sobbed. 'Hurts.'

Peter just assumed that he had bruised himself again and that the pain would go away, but it didn't.

'Hurts, Mummy. Hurts Mummy. Daddy, *hurts*.'

Michael never complained unless something was wrong, and after another day of watching his son in pain, Peter felt a sickness in his stomach. He called Dr James, who in turn took the call seriously because he knew Peter was never one to exaggerate. In his surgery he gingerly examined Michael's shin.

'Some bruising,' he said. 'He could have a splintered shin. An X-ray is the only way to sort this out. I'll ring Reading and organise it. I'm pretty sure it will be a cracked bone.'

But of course it wasn't. Two days later, Peter and Anne sat nervously in the consulting room at the hospital while Mum stayed anxiously at home with a miserable Michael. Peter knew it was bad news when the consultant paediatrician carefully avoided their eyes.

'I am dreadfully sorry. I don't know how to say this, so I'll have to give it to you straight. Michael is seriously ill. He has a sarcoma in his right tibia. But it *is* curable if we act quickly.'

Anne clutched her husband, and Peter's cancer expertise clicked in.

'An osteosarcoma in a child his age. Surely that's impossible. I thought it only happened in teenage children.'

The consultant looked back at them in sorrow.

'I'm truly sorry Mr Stott. Truly. But it does happen. It's incredibly rare in a child of his age. It's Nature being horrible. But I'm as sure as dammit that it is an osteosarcoma. I just wish I'm wrong. But I'm not.'

'So what's going to happen?' whispered Anne.

'We have to act quickly,' said the paediatrician. 'The only effective option is surgery.'

'Surgery?' Anne could barely speak.

'The leg has to come off. Below the knee.'

'Oh my God.'

Ann collapsed against Peter's chest, sobbing, while her distraught husband forced himself to ask the next question.

'When?'

'As soon as possible. We'll get a cure if we act now. It's in its early stages and his chances are really good. And I mean that. We must act quickly and I'll need your permission.' He indicated a form on his desk. 'If you sign this we can have him in on Thursday as an emergency admission.'

All this was too much for Anne. She just clung to her husband.

'Could I have a moment with my wife?' asked Peter

'Of course,' said the paediatrician. 'I'll go get a coffee and come back in about ten minutes.' He stopped. 'Mr and Mrs Stott, I have a son about your son's age. If he had this condition, my advice would be the same. I know this is horrible and unfair, but it has to be done.' He hesitated again, forcing himself to be brutal. 'A lost leg is better than a lost life.'

It was a long ten minutes, and during that time Peter managed to get through to Anne.

'Darling, we have to do it. It's the only way to save him. If we don't do it, it will spread fast. Cancer does that in growing children. Without the operation he'd have only months.'

After that Anne shed more tears, but by the time the consultant returned she had accepted reality. She had just one more question for him.

'So when his—the leg is off. What then? Will he have to have a…?'

'Prosthesis. False leg. No. Not at present. We'll leave him with a stump and he'll have to use crutches which are adjustable to cope with his growth. That will give us time to make sure the stump is well fleshed and ready for use when he needs a new leg. If it is not, we'll deal with that with a small operation. But for the next couple of years, it will be crutches. You'd be surprised how quickly they pick it up.'

'Really?' asked Anne.

'Oh yes,' said the paediatrician. 'Do come and have a quick look at our children's ward.'

So he took the Stotts down the corridor where they saw a three-year-old victim of a road crash, cheerfully bombing along on his crutches.

'Been here six weeks,' said the consultant. 'Nearly dead when he came in. Now look at him.'

Anne was satisfied.

'Thank you, Doctor,' she said bleakly. 'We are ready to sign now.'

'Fine. I'll ring your Dr James and ask for morphine and sedation till Thursday.'

That evening following Dr James's visit, Michael was quietly asleep and in no pain. His parents and grandmother sat forlornly around the kitchen table, putting a brave face on things and trying to encourage each other to eat. In bed that night Anne and Peter clung to each other, alternately sobbing and talking, and unable to sleep. Every hour they checked Michael, who was unconscious due to the heavy sedation

The next day they packed a small bag of his things, and with his favourite teddy they took him to hospital where he was again given a sedative and morphine. Anne stayed with him as long as possible and then left in tears. That night, sleep again was impossible for the parents and grandmother. Michael was first in theatre next morning, and by eleven it was all over.

At half past, the ward sister came into the waiting room and smiled directly at them.

'Good news, Mr and Mrs Stott. The operation went well and he's coming through it without any problems. You can see him now.'

She led them into the ward and up to a small white cot. A waxen faced Michael was lying on his back, his lower body covered with what looked like a small garden cloche under a blanket. Blood dripped steadily into his arm from a bottle, but, thank God, he was breathing steadily.

'He's such a beautiful child,' said the sister enthusiastically.

He *was*, thought Peter savagely, now he's just a boy aged one and a half with one and a half legs.

But he dismissed such thoughts as he took Michael's hand and Anne kissed her son on his forehead. Both tried to avert their eyes from that awful cloche while they waited until Michael finally opened his eyes. He just smiled his mother's beautiful smile and said 'Mummy' while his parents tried to blink back their tears and smile back. The worst was over.

Michael quickly became the apple of the nurses' eye. They either had children or wished they had a toddler as attractive as him, and he quickly became their favourite and was spoilt rotten. Anne and Peter visited him every day, and Susan went to see him after a week.

'Lady Susan,' he said, beaming at her and trying out his new words. 'Blood. Bandage.' He pointed at his stump. 'Leg gone'

Susan smiled back, trying not to weep.

'Yes, Michael, leg gone.'

Despite her tears Susan was happy to see how well he looked and also relieved to know that the operation had been successful. She was also worried that Michael's fall might have exacerbated the problem, but Peter put her right.

'It was nothing to do with you, Susan,' he said. 'The cancer was there. The fall just made it painful. It's ridiculous really. They usually find osteosarcoma in kids during their growth spurt. Teenagers usually. But Michael is growing fast, and so it got him early. As one of the specialists said, one of Nature's jokes.'

Susan said nothing. Jokes were meant to be funny.

Michael was in hospital for just over three weeks. During the first week he had to be restrained to stop him damaging his stump. By the second he was trying to haul himself upwards using the bars of his cot, and in his third week he was standing, holding the bars like a caged animal. As he could stand with support, the staff decided to free him and he was allowed to take a few faltering steps on his crutches with the support of the ward sister and Anne. Mum looked on anxiously, but Michael did really well. Three days after that he was allowed home.

Mum went back to Mull and Anne stopped all painting and devoted herself to her son. Peter went back to work, where Susan updated him with the latest from Thirsk.

'They want a final meeting on Friday, to discuss their options again.'

There were really only two main possibilities. Thirsk could continue to finance research into the mode of action of cytocide with a view to modifying the molecule to remove its anti-pancreatic effect, but that could be hugely expensive, though the pay-off would be colossal if they succeeded. The alternative was to try to sell the patent, with its proven anti-cancer properties, to another company with an expertise in drug modification. Glaxo had already shown in an interest. Thirsk asked if MICR would do the research for them, but Director Stephens was firm about that.

'We are, and will remain, a research institute,' he said. 'Cytocide was supposed to be a one-off diversion into drug testing. And you have paid us well for it. But that's it. No more testing. If I were you I'd take up the Glaxo offer. You'll get your money back plus a good profit.'

The Thirsk directors all agreed with him, and Stephens added a request.

'In the interim, Dr Pearce would like to carry out work on the anti-cancer properties of cytocide. The results would be available to everyone, including Glaxo. Would that be okay?'

It was.

At home, Anne was worrying about Michael. The hospital had said that they couldn't risk him damaging his stump in a fall and had fitted him with a protective "cage" which covered the wound and strapped on above the knee. Michael hated it and refused to wear it. Eventually Anne lost patience.

'If you want to get up, you put on your cage. Otherwise you stay in bed.'

'Stay bed,' said Michael rebelliously.

So Anne tucked him down firmly, and bolted his cot to make sure he couldn't get out. After half an hour of screaming, Michael gave in.

'Want get up, Mummy. Want get *up*.'

'With your cage,' insisted Anne

'Get up cage.'

Having accepted the indignity of his cage, Michael quickly forgot about it as he moved along cautiously on his crutches. He was a quick learner and fearless, and Anne was pleased with his progress, but after almost an hour dragging himself around he was exhausted and retired to his cot for a nap, while Anne rested on the sofa. She was tired, but happy. It was going to be alright; Michael was coping well and Peter would be delighted to see his progress when he got home, but before he arrived there was another problem to be dealt with. The district nurse was coming over to dress Michael's stump and to show his mother how to do it in the future. Anne was already dreading the experience; she hated blood and hated looking at her son's amputation. But it had to be done.

'Lovely,' said the nurse, looking at the lump of pink flesh. 'No bruising, no infection. All looks good. Just keep on with the padding, and he'll be fine. Not too tight, and certainly not too loose. See here.'

Anne tried to stop the gall rising in her throat and with a huge effort she wound the padding around the pink horror.

'Mummy do,' said Michael in amazement.

'Mummy do well,' grinned the nurse. 'You're doing fine, Mrs Stott, really well done.'

After that Anne had a huge gin and tonic while Mike had his afternoon nap.

During the following months things gradually reverted to a form of normality. Susan returned to the main institute to work with Deirdre Pearce, and the facilities at Clerkenwell were sold off as a part of Ciencia's bankruptcy. She and Alice visited Maidenhead regularly and were delighted at Michael's progress. He had become totally proficient on his crutches, which had to be adjusted regularly to cope with his growth. He was speaking coherently and had already caught his first small fish from the river. Anne started painting again; her first picture was from her "dark" period, with a heavy death symbolism, but she gradually reverted back to normal with her beautifully emotive riverscapes.

Mum came down from Scotland to celebrate Michael's second birthday, and after she and Michael had cut the cake, Peter proposed a toast:

'To Michael, and the NHS.'

Chapter 10
Betrayal

Aunt Alice was driving down the M4, trying to keep the A35 at a steady fifty and looking for the Maidenhead turnoff. It was the first week of January and they were travelling back from a New Year do in Bath. The day was cold, with snowflakes on the wind, but they were determined to stop off at the Presbyterian Church. And there it was, in stark simplicity, a small black headstone with gold letters:

> Michael Samuel Stott
> Beloved son of Anne and Peter
> Born 28th July 1964
> Died 31st October 1966

Susan put a bunch of Scillonian daffodils on the grave, then stepped back and hugged Alice. Together they walked back through the snow to the car. Alice suggested that they might stop in at the Stotts to offer their condolences, but Susan vetoed that.

'Just leave them to it. They've enough on their plate.'

They did indeed. Christmas and the New Year had been agony for Peter, Anne and Mum. Anne was on autopilot doing everything necessary, but immersed in her loss and her resentment of Peter's actions. The atmosphere had become so poisonous that Peter had returned to work directly after New Year's Day, and so he wouldn't have been at home had Alice and Susan arrived.

It had been early August when they had realised that the cancer had spread. In a horrid repeat performance, Michael used the same words as before:

'It hurts, Mummy. Hurts.'

'Where?'

Michael poked his lower back, and Anne looked at it. No bruising, no sponginess, and the pain eventually went, but in two days it was back.

'Hurts, Daddy, *hurts.*'

It was with huge trepidation that they went back to the paediatrician, but Peter knew the outcome long before the X-ray results were explained to them. The cancer had spread to Mike's pelvis and spine. No hope, three months at best.

After a day of tears and desolation, Anne hardened up her act.

'Peter, we have to do *something.* We can't just sit back and watch him die.'

Possibly that's best, thought Peter, *just keep up the morphine and let him die without pain.*

But instead he said, 'Like what?'

'You're the cancer expert.'

'But nothing cures bone cancer, Anne.'

'You don't know that. Wouldn't cytocide work?'

'It might.'

'So why not try it?' persisted Anne. 'It worked on Janet Team. It might well work on Michael. It might cure him, or at least, give him more time.'

'And it will give him pancreatitis,' said Peter firmly. 'I wouldn't wish that death sentence on *anyone.*'

'But it only gave pancreatitis in a few rats,' screamed Anne. 'For God's sake, Peter, this is our son we're talking about. I can't believe you won't do it.'

Peter's real reason for not wanting to inject cytocide was that Mike had been truly traumatised in hospital and was terrified of injections. As a loving father, Peter hated the idea of inflicting any pain on his son, and so he resisted Anne's furious nagging for almost two weeks before giving in and reluctantly bringing home the drug. In the rat trial with cytocide the animals had been injected intramuscularly, and Peter continued the same procedure with his son, but it was worse than he anticipated, because Mike had a huge screaming fit every time Peter stuck the laden syringe into his small behind.

In the two months after his diagnosis, Mike lost a little weight but otherwise seemed well. Anne gave him painkillers when he complained, but otherwise he seemed happy. Peter took to giving him his injections in the early morning when he was still asleep, but the prick still woke him into a terrorised screaming session.

'It has to be that way,' said Anne firmly. 'We have to be cruel to be kind.'

Cruel is the word, thought Peter, but he reluctantly carried on.

Then fate struck its cruellest blow of all. Mike suddenly started wobbling on his crutches and fell over a number of times. A further X-ray showed the reality, that the tumour was now pressing on his spinal cord and paralysing his legs. Peter knew it was the end; even if a miracle happened and Mike survived he would never walk again. Time to let him go.

Michael was miserable, but not apparently in pain. He tried dragging himself along on his bottom, screaming with fury at not being able to walk. Finally Dr James had to sedate him and confined him to his cot where he dozed fitfully. Anne forced the reluctant Peter to continue the injections, which were now easy because Michael had lost all sensation in his buttocks.

Peter had hoped that Anne would accept the reality of Michael's mortality, but she had other ideas. She had spent a huge amount of time reading up everything on cancer treatment and had homed in on a clinic in Switzerland which claimed good results using a high protein diet coupled with enormous vitamin supplementation and hyperbaric therapy.

'I think we should give it a try,' she said firmly. 'You know we can afford it.'

'I know we can. That's not the point, Anne. Darling, he's going. For Christ's sake, just let him die in peace at home. All Switzerland's giving is false hope.'

'Any hope's better than none.'

'I've given up hope,' said Peter. 'Anne, Mike is dying. Accept it. The Swiss' so-called method is ridiculous. It's a joke. It's not even scientific.'

'I don't believe it,' screamed Anne. 'You're actually sacrificing our son over some *scientific principle*?'

As before, Peter held out against Anne's fury, but only for a week. Eventually she telegraphed the clinic, and they replied saying that they could take Michael in about a week when they had a "vacancy". Delighted, she booked the flight to Zurich.

By now, Michael's condition had seriously worsened: he was now as thin as a rail and resembled a comatose old man. Dr James thought that the trip would kill him, and in an unspoken agreement with Peter, he gradually increased the doses of morphine until Michael fell quietly into his last sleep.

After Christmas, Anne was still on autopilot. She prepared Peter's breakfast, painted all day, and had supper on the table when he arrived home. Conversation was desultory, as was their sex, with none of the joy of before. Anne went firmly on the Pill and refused to talk about Michael. She continued her interest in cancer, and even came up to the Institute to "look things up" in the library. She also had lunch with Susan who gave her a tour of the newly refurbished facilities. Her painting was now truly in her "dark" phase, a master class in death, with villagers dancing around gibbets instead of maypoles. The gallery sold her oils as fast as she could produce them.

Susan watched the gradual dissolution of Peter's marriage with mixed feelings. She had finally admitted to her friends that she was in love with Peter. No surprise there, they'd known it for years. She also knew that Peter was still in love with Anne and desperately trying to hold on, and so she decided to play the long game. Be a supportive friend and colleague, make no move until the time was right.

Events came to a head that June, when Anne decided to take a holiday alone with Mum in Scotland.

'I have to get away,' she said. 'I need some space and time to think. I'll do some sketching up there. I imagine you'll be okay?'

Peter had to agree. He had no choice.

He was totally miserable for the next three weeks, and began to wonder if Anne would ever return. She did, but only to collect her things and the MG.

'I'm leaving you, Peter. I've thought it all through. I'm sorry, but I can't live with you anymore. Not after Michael. I'm beginning to hate you.'

'You don't mean that.'

'Yes, I do. If you need to get in touch you can write to me at Mum's.'

133

Peter watched white faced as she piled her cases into the car before asking the ultimate question:

'Anne, there's no one else, is there?'

'Of course not.'

With that the MG swirled down the drive.

Peter shed tears that night and was late into work the next morning. He didn't mention Anne to anyone and they all thought she was still on holiday in Scotland. At home that evening he confronted the breakfast things in an empty kitchen and realised that things had changed forever. He wrote a letter to Anne with a cheque to help her out and received a belated and curt 'thank you' two weeks later. By then the staff at MICR had realised that Anne and he had separated, and most were genuinely upset and assumed the marriage was doomed. Susan was quietly elated; things were going her way.

During the next few months Peter lived a subdued bachelor life. He wrote to Anne every month with a cheque, and always got a reply, which gave him hope. She always took weeks to answer, but Peter assumed that the postal service to Mull was as awful as ever. Meanwhile the gallery in Marlow kept asking for more of Anne's pictures and Peter wrote to see if she wanted to sell those that were in the house. She said 'no' and that she was now with a new gallery in Glasgow which had its headquarters in London.

Things took a turn for the better in October while Peter was at a pharmaceutical conference in Oxford. At his table was an attractive woman who he vaguely recognised. She smiled at him and he smiled back.

'Hello,' he said. 'I'm Peter Stott.'

'I know,' she replied, smiling. 'Your fame precedes you. You are the scientific sleuth, the Sherlock Holmes of the cancer world.'

Peter laughed. 'That I was. Now I'm just an ordinary biochemist.'

After the meeting they had an evening meal, and Louise returned home to her husband who was an executive in Glaxo. It took several more meetings before their affair began. They were not in love with each other; Louise was still enamoured with her neglectful husband while Peter still grieved over his absent wife, and so their attraction was purely sexual.

In early November the weather was awful, and Peter was hugely depressed on the anniversary of Mike's death. To cheer himself up he decided on a little retail therapy. His father had been a jeweller, and Peter had a keen interest in antique silver. For years he had wanted to own a complete set of silver apostle spoons, but genuine spoons from the 1600s cost a fortune. He'd seen the Christie's advert in the Telegraph, and included in the list of goodies was a complete set of thirteen Victorian spoons. Not the real thing, just 19th century copies, but they would be a start.

So it was with pleasurable anticipation that Peter strolled down St James to Christies, and it was with amazement that he gazed into the window of one of the posher art galleries. There in pride of place was one of Anne's paintings, an oil of a spectral landscape with a canal in the foreground and with a staggering price of two hundred guineas. Peter didn't recognise the scene; it certainly wasn't on the Thames and he assumed Anne had painted it from a photograph as she often did. In Christies, as he looked carefully at the spoons (estimate sixty guineas) he wondered irritably if his wife still needed her monthly cheque as she seemed to be doing rather well without it.

At last Christmas dragged itself around again and Peter got cards and letters from both Mum and Anne. Mum's letter was encouraging; she had always liked Peter and was hugely upset by the rift in the marriage. She told him in confidence that Anne had ruled out divorce, and that gave him a huge burst of hope. Anne's letter was equally encouraging. Was he looking after himself? Was he eating properly? Yes, the art was selling pretty well, thank you very much. And thanks for the regular cheques. Her concern touched him; the letter was the best present he could have had. Out of loyalty to her he cancelled a previously planned assignation with Louise for the coming weekend.

Susan and Alice were also concerned about Peter, and after much discussion and agonising Susan asked her boss whether he would like to come over to Ilford for lunch on Christmas Day. To her astonishment he accepted cheerfully, and was the life and soul of the party. Susan wore her beautiful new dress and new perfume to create an effect, but all she got was a peck on the cheek as Peter left. So much for Chanel No. 5

The next step in the marital reconciliation was a formal invitation, on a gold edged card, to the April opening of an exhibition of Anne's pictures in London. Peter arrived at the gallery late, shaking with nerves and wondering how he would speak to Anne. In practice she made it easy for him, leaving the group she was talking to and coming straight over to him. She gave him a smile and a peck on the cheek.

'Peter, it's you. It's lovely to see you again.'

'And you. Thanks for inviting me. It's all very impressive.'

She's not changed, he thought. *Still as beautiful as ever. But slimmer.* As he looked at her she turned to an elegantly dressed man on her left.

'Peter, this is John Jamieson, the owner of the gallery. John, this is my husband Peter.'

Peter was delighted to be called husband.

'Glad to meet you, Peter. You have a talented wife. Truly talented. There's been a huge amount of interest.' He indicated the well-heeled group with their champagne glasses. 'We've already sold six.'

Peter didn't want to talk to Jamieson; he was there for Anne, but she was already mixing with the clients. He moved closer to her, at the same time looking at the oils. They were all dark, with gaunt figures, jagged trees and ruined buildings. Two were of the canal scene he'd seen before, and some had Scottish mountains in the background. He'd seen this new style after the murders of Lomax and Team; he hadn't liked it then and he didn't like it now, but the murmurs of admiration around him made him realise that he was in a minority. Anne was in the centre of it all, lapping up the praise and seemingly oblivious to his presence. That continued all evening, with Peter being forced to mix with the guests while trying desperately to talk to his wife. Finally, after a long wait, the crowd diminished and Anne came over and gave him one of her beautiful smiles.

'I am taking the night sleeper to Glasgow,' she said. 'We could go for a coffee now and then take the Tube to Euston.'

'That would be really nice,' said Peter in amazement.

So they had an extensive espresso together, while Anne talked about life in Scotland.

'It's lovely in Mull in the summer, but the winter days are so short. So different from down here.'

'You don't *have* to stay there,' said Peter, choosing his words carefully.

Anne looked him straight in the eye.

'I know,' she said. 'Just give me more time to think, Peter.'

'Take as much time as you want.'

To enhance his hopes he got a kiss at Euston as she got on the train.

After that meeting their correspondence became more frequent, and in his final letter Peter finally emptied his heart.

My darling Anne,

I miss you terribly; you always were and still are the love of my life. We both loved Michael. I still think of him every day as I think of you. But being apart will not bring him back. Please forgive me for anything I may have done to hurt you, and do come back home soon. Please write.

Your loving husband, Peter.

Three days later, his letter arrived in Mull. Anne opened it and nodded. She didn't want a divorce, even though she knew she couldn't forget all the past arguments and the delays in treating Michael, but life had to go on, and she had plans for a new version back in Maidenhead. Finally, she put pen to paper.

My dear Peter,

I'm coming back if you'll have me. If it's all right with you, I'll drive down Wednesday next week and stay overnight in Carlisle. So I should be there by evening on that Friday. I'll phone you at six on Saturday to check that this is all okay. I'm really looking forward to seeing the house again.

Love Anne.

When Peter got the Saturday phone call he almost wept with relief when he heard that she really was coming back. He was so happy that he didn't ask her why she was stopping off in Carlisle instead of her usual York.

Peter took three days holiday in the week that Anne was due to return. He got in a cleaning lady, and together they scoured the house from top to bottom. By Thursday evening the place was immaculate, with flowers in every room and fresh fish in the refrigerator. Anne actually arrived late that Friday afternoon, and Peter's eyes filled with relief as he saw the MG swing up the drive. He rushed out and hugged her delightedly as she got out of the car, and she hugged him back in turn and gave him a kiss on the mouth. Then she pulled back.

'You've really kept the garden nice, Peter.'

He smiled back.

'I've tried to keep on top of it. And the house too.' He took her hand and led her into the hall. 'You'll see it's the same as ever. 'It certainly is. You look around while I get in your stuff.'

As Anne went slowly through house and garden, Peter took the suitcases up to the spare bedroom, then went down to find his wife sitting on the seat by the river. He approached her hesitantly.

'Anne, I've put your stuff in the back bedroom,' he said. 'I thought you might like some time to yourself before—'

Anne gave him her best smile.

'Peter dear, I didn't come back to Maidenhead to live like a nun. We'll be together in our old room.'

Peter gave her a delighted kiss.

That evening they made love like never before. Peter had never encountered such ferocity; it was the first time he had female nails draw blood on his back. Their sex was primeval and savage, leaving Peter both elated and shocked.

The next day they had lunch in Marlow, and Anne went back to her old gallery where they were delighted to see their old exhibitor, who had received a fine review in The Times. Next morning Peter went back to work, leaving Anne to get her bearings and re-establish contact with her friends in Maidenhead.

The first person Peter bumped into at the Institute was Deirdre Pearce, who was delighted to hear that Anne had returned home.

'I'm really glad for you Peter. You've been so unhappy without her. It's been a terrible time for you both, and now you look so elated.'

'Thanks Deirdre.' He gave her a peck on the cheek.

After that the news spread like wildfire, and so Susan had an answer ready for when she met up with Peter. With a huge effort she smiled and said that she was happy for them both. That night, in the solitude of her bedroom, she sobbed herself to sleep in the certain knowledge that all was lost.

Life in Maidenhead soon settled down into a routine. When they were first married Anne had been the housewife, keeping scientific husband fed and watered while dabbling in painting, but things had changed, and Peter realised belatedly that Anne too had a career and encouraged her to paint even more. She in return supplied him with good food prepared by an expert cook. Their roles had reversed: Anne was now in control, but Peter didn't mind that because he was so delighted to have her back. At first he was irritated at her control of their sex life; previously if he had wanted to make love she would have acquiesced quite willingly. Not anymore. Sex was only on the cards when she wanted it and that was not often, and Peter had to accept the status quo. It was a small price to pay for having her at home, and he was happy. Michael and pregnancy were not discussed.

Susan finally had to accept the fact that Peter could not be a full part of her life in the way that she wanted. She would never be Mrs Susan Stott, or even the lover of Dr Peter Stott. She had long tearful discussions with Aunt Alice who suggested that the only long-term solution was to leave the Institute and look for other men. Susan half-heartedly tried out some new boyfriends, but she found none satisfactory on the basis of either their intellectual or sexual prowess. Finally, in August, she desperately started applying for scientific jobs in Australia and the USA, with the long term aim of emigrating and getting Peter completely out of her system.

Like Peter, Anne had her daily routine. She painted each day while she was at home and went out sketching and photographing one or two days a week. Thursday became the perennial away-day, weather permitting, because Peter almost always had afternoon conferences and was almost always home late. And it was on a Thursday in September that Peter was given a clue that all was not what it seemed. He'd arrived home at seven that evening to find neither Anne nor the MG at home, and she'd arrived about half an hour later explaining that she had been sketching near Goring lock and found that the car wouldn't start. The AA had arrived, diagnosed a faulty starter motor and towed it to a garage in Reading.

'That was quite a long tow,' said Peter admiringly.

'Yes it was. But they got me there, they were very good. Then I walked the station and came home. They say they may not get it done until after the weekend.'

'Which garage?'

'Anderson's.'

The loss of the car was only a minor irritation, as they had planned a quiet weekend, with Anne finishing off a recent commission and Peter trying to tie up the loose ends of a scientific paper he was to present next Wednesday. Things didn't go to plan and he rushed into work early on Monday to frantically prepare some extra slides with Susan. That done, he went home exhausted and decided to lie in and have a day off before tomorrow's big conference. So that morning he was still asleep at ten when the phone rang, and he picked up the receiver in the bedroom at exactly the same time as Anne in the kitchen.

'I've told you not to call me here,' she hissed. 'He's here, still in bed. What on earth do you want?'

'Sorry darling. Anderson's rang. They say the car's done. You want me to collect it?'

'Yes please, now get off the telephone. Don't call me again. You know what we agreed.'

The phone clicked downstairs, while Peter lay in bed holding the receiver. Eventually he heard Anne coming upstairs and he carefully replaced the receiver in its cradle before she came in with his cup of tea.

'Who was that on the phone?' he asked, trying to control his pounding heart and furious disbelief.

'Just Anderson's. Saying the car's ready.'

As with Ron Team, the first lie. And as with his former colleague, there would be a lot more.

'Good,' he said.

'You look pale,' she observed. 'Are you alright?'

'My stomach's churning,' he said truthfully. Then he lied. 'Must have been that fish last night.'

'Nonsense,' she smiled. 'I don't cook bad fish.'

For the rest of the day Peter pretended to be working on his presentation while Anne pottered in her studio. His mind initially was a confused mixture of fury and anxiety, but finally his questioning brain took over. Who the hell was her lover? His only clue was the connection with Anderson's, and Peter started there. He got the number from directory enquiries, rang it and asked to speak to the chief mechanic.

'I'd just like to say how much we appreciate you dealing with our MG so promptly. We didn't expect such good service and we are really very grateful.'

The mechanic was puzzled. 'It's very nice to be thanked,' he said. 'But I think you must have the wrong branch. We haven't seen any MGs recently, but it could be our other place in Woolhampton. You must have got the wrong number.'

Woolhampton. Peter knew vaguely where it was, and the Ordnance Survey confirmed it was west of Reading, with a rail link, and adjacent to the abandoned Kennet and Avon Canal. His memory banks slowly stirred and he remembered Anne's pictures in London with a derelict canal in the foreground. He now knew he had to pay the village an urgent visit, but that could only come after the conference tomorrow.

Peter and Susan met at Euston station early next morning. Susan was nervous as it would be a big day for her. She would be presenting her first small paper and she had to wait anxiously all day until her moment of glory in the evening session. It was all over in a quarter of an hour, and she received a genuine round of applause. In the bar afterwards Peter temporarily forgot his problems at home and bought two brandies. He handed Susan hers and they clinked glasses, and he bowed to her in mock admiration.

'Well done Miss Preston. Well done indeed. You knocked them dead.' He gave her a congratulatory kiss on the cheek.

Susan gulped her brandy.

'And thank you Peter. I'd have never done it if you hadn't encouraged me.' With a sudden rush of alcoholic courage she returned his peck on the cheek. He grinned back.

'Thank you for that.'

They chatted casually for a few minutes, but Peter's worries inevitably returned and the conversation stalled. With yet another brandy he became morose. Susan could see that he was worried and anxious, and the brandy again gave her the courage to ask a question.

'Peter, what's the matter? Have I done something wrong?'

For a moment he let his guard down.

'No, it's not you. Just some trouble at home.'

'Anne?'

'Yes, she's…acting oddly.'

Susan didn't push her luck by asking how, but her curiosity was fully aroused. Peter's guard was now fully up, and he did not elaborate.

Next morning Susan and Peter took the train back to London. Neither spoke much, and at Euston Susan continued on to the Institute while Peter went to Paddington and then on to Reading. There, he took a slow train to Woolhampton, where he found Anderson's garage. He didn't go in and ask about Anne's car because he thought it might arouse suspicion. Instead he asked directions to the canal, and as he emerged from a small clump of trees he saw the scene that would be riveted in his brain for ever. Anne had got it just right in her oil: a disused lock with a walkway over the gates, various old huts obviously used by the previous canal operators and water spewing gently out of the lock gate. Some distance down the canal was a brick cottage set well back from the old tow path and obviously occupied with a shirt flapping gently on the clothes line. On the nearside of the canal, just off the track, and neatly parked in some bushes was Anne's MG.

Peter sat down in shock. His gorge rose in his mouth and he thought he might be sick, but as the taste of bile subsided his rage took over. That bitch, that lying, betraying cow. But rage alone was not enough, he had to know it *all*. He forced himself to think rationally and found a spot near the village where he could keep the cottage under surveillance. Apart from a few anglers the canal was deserted, and it wasn't until late afternoon that Anne's familiar figure emerged from the cottage, waved happily and walked carefully over the lock gates. With a familiar growl the MG moved off.

Anne was busy preparing supper when Peter arrived home some two hours later. She gave him a kiss on the cheek.

'Had a good day? How was the conference?'

'It went well. We both did our talks and got a lot of interest. I was very pleased. How about you, what have you been doing since I last saw you?'

'Just some pottering and painting today, and some cooking.'

The war of lies was intensifying.

The final truth was revealed to Peter the following week. He returned to Woolhampton armed with his fishing rod and tackle in the certain knowledge that Anne would not be there as she had a prearranged meeting with Jamieson at the gallery in London. At the canal, he carefully sat down within earshot of an elderly angler who was catching a few tench, and Peter gently chatted about the fishing and carefully swung the conversation around to the canal and its residents. After they'd shared a couple of bottles of Guinness he had most of the facts he needed.

'Who's lucky enough to live in that pretty cottage?'

'That's Ian Stuart. Lived here for years. He's a specialist woodcarver, I think he works mainly for the Church.'

'Any family?'

'He's actually a widower and he's got a daughter, but she doesn't live with him. They say she works in London somewhere, but I've never seen her. I only took up fishing here about a year ago. Apparently, the daughter moved out when the girlfriend moved in.'

Peter carefully digested all these facts before continuing.

'Has he always lived there?'

'Oh yes, I think so. But about a year ago he rented out the cottage when he went north to do some work up there. Someone told me Newcastle. Or was it Carlisle? Then he came back here with her. Ah, there's a bite.'

He struck and pulled in yet another tench, and during the next ten minutes he reeled in another five. As Peter silently watched the fish drop into the keepnet, he tried to sequence Anne's ultimate betrayal, and when the fish stopped biting, he asked a few more carefully selected questions. He then had it all, and the complete story produced a total sense of humiliation and betrayal which reinforced his raging hatred. He now knew with absolute certainty that Anne had started the affair before she left him, had been seeing Stuart in Carlisle on and off when she was supposedly based on Mull and continued the relationship when she came back to him in Maidenhead. He thought long and hard on the train home, and by the time he opened the front door his thoughts had fused into an implacable desire for revenge. *That* was a dish best served cold, and he would serve his with ice.

The beautiful blue-eyed betrayer would have to go.

Chapter 11
Death — Where Is Thy Sting?

Peter knew that when a married woman met an unexplained death, the first suspicions would be directed at her husband. He knew he had to make sure that Anne's death appeared accidental, and he had to have a cast iron alibi for the day in question. The first problem was relatively easily dealt with: her lover's house was just a few hundred yards from an abandoned lock and quick slip on wet stone by a non-swimmer could easily cause a tragedy. The alibi was the main problem, and he racked his brains for weeks to find an answer. The first glimmerings of a solution came when he was visiting the microbiology unit at University College where his friend Alan Jones was working on bacterial toxins.

'It's an odd thing about these endotoxins,' said Alan. 'There's such a huge difference between the amount that will make you ill and the amount that will kill you.'

Peter pricked up his ears.

'What do you mean by that?'

'Well, the lethal dose will give you profound bloody diarrhoea and a huge fever, and so you'll die most unpleasantly. But if you take only a hundredth of the dose you'll get a hell of a fever and a little diarrhoea and it won't kill you. Actually, I shouldn't say "you", we've only tested it on rats and rabbits.'

'How do you get these toxins?' asked Peter.

'We extract them. We grow the E. coli in these—' he indicated a large jar which was being stirred by motor, 'then we harvest the bugs and extract the toxin from the cell walls. That's it here.' He picked up a bottle off his desk and showed Peter the white powder inside. 'That's the toxin, perfectly safe as long as you don't get it inside you.' He put the bottle back on his desk and moved towards the door. 'Come on, I'll show you the animals.'

The animal room was full of white rabbits, most in large spacious cages, but about ten of them were in tiny individual cages, with each animal restrained with a strap. They all had an electrical thermometer in their rectum and their internal temperatures were being continuously recorded on a rolling chart.

'We've just finished our tests,' said Alan. 'And we're just about to take out the thermometers and put the animals back into their usual cages. See, their temperatures are all normal.' He indicated the recorder. 'But watch. I'll give this one just one microgram of the toxin.'

He selected an ampoule and drew some liquid out of it with a syringe.

Then he selected a rabbit, rubbed some alcohol on its ear and injected the liquid into its prominent ear vein.

'We'll leave it for about half an hour while we have a cup of tea,' he said. 'Then we'll come back and see what's happened. At the moment, its temperature is 38.8 degrees. That's normal.'

They went to the Institute's canteen for about three quarters of an hour. When they returned Peter saw that the condition of the injected animal had changed completely. Before the injection it had been clear eyed with smooth fur, but now its fur was staring and the eyes were dull. It was clearly ill. Alan pointed to the recording.

'There you are,' he said. 'Its temperature is 40.7. Up almost two degrees. The toxin has a huge pyrogenic effect. Sends the temperature up like a rocket, then after about two hours it'll start coming right down.'

'So you can generate a temperature virtually at will?'

'Yes,' replied Alan. 'I suppose we can.'

The germ of an idea was forming in Peter's brain. Later, as he watched the work in the lab, he backed up to Alan's desk and quietly slid the bottle of toxin into his pocket.

'I'm just off to the toilet,' he said. 'See you in a minute.'

In the cubicle Peter carefully unscrewed the lid of the bottle and tipped a small amount of the white powder into a spare envelope he had in his pocket. He folded it up carefully so that it wouldn't leak and then went back to the lab. While Alan was

145

giving instructions to a technician he carefully put the bottle back onto his colleague's desk and made his farewells.

'Thank you so much, Alan. It's been really fascinating.'

Back in his own laboratory Peter sat down and thought. One microgram of the toxin had produced a fever in a rabbit and that would be equivalent to a dose of about 70 micrograms in an average man. As a scientist he knew that the response to drugs varied hugely between animals, and he knew he had to be cautious. Start with a low dose, and work up. He put on mask and gloves and carefully weighed out 100 milligrams of the toxin. The amount was so small that it barely covered the end of his spatula. He tipped it into a beaker, added 100 millilitres of saline and stirred the liquid with a glass rod. The clear solution now contained 1000 micrograms of toxin in each millilitre, and just one millilitre would be more than sufficient to kill a rabbit. This would be his stock solution; he would have to dilute it down before he could risk sticking it into his own arm.

He waited until the weekend before injecting himself. On Saturday morning he went into the garage, opened the fridge where he kept his biological samples and took out the bottle of diluted toxin. He lowered his trousers, sucked up the toxin into a syringe and jammed it into his thigh. Shaking with apprehension he went back into the house, where Anne noticed the sweat on his forehead.

'You look awful,' she said. 'What's the matter? Are you ill?'

'I've got a bit of a pain in the stomach,' he replied, anticipating the sickness to come.

'So where is it hurting?'

'Here.' He prodded under his ribs where he thought the pain would come. 'Probably that liver last night.'

In practice nothing happened. By mid-morning, Peter realised that the toxin had hardly affected him, and he was almost certain that he knew why. He had injected himself intramuscularly, while the rabbits in Alan's lab had received the toxin directly into their bloodstream via a vein. He could have injected himself the same way, but he didn't want any tell-tale injection marks on his arms, and so he knew that if he was going to continue injecting intramuscularly he'd have to increase the dose to get an effect. He would try again tomorrow.

Anne was going to visit her old gallery on Sunday and so he waited until she had gone before injecting himself again. This time he used ten times as much toxin. Within half an hour he felt slightly queasy and after a full hour he had a headache and was sweating. His bowels were loose and so he had to rush to the toilet to empty them, and while he was in the bathroom he checked his temperature. It was up almost a degree, and so he crawled into bed. He was still there when Anne arrived home.

'So where's it hurting?'

Peter poked himself gingerly under his ribs.

'That's not good,' she said. 'Temperature, diarrhoea and pain. If it was just a normal stomach upset you wouldn't have any temperature.'

Peter was irritated at Anne playing the professional nurse.

'It's only a small temperature, and it's almost gone now.' He looked straight into her beautiful blue eyes, seeing what he thought were genuine signs of concern, and for a moment he was tempted to change his course of action. Then he remembered the love nest by the lock, and hardened his resolve. The tests with the toxin would go on.

It took almost six weeks of intermittent testing before Peter cracked the problem. An injection of two hundred micrograms would produce a fever within an hour of the injection and the fake illness would last up to three hours. He found that he could control the diarrhoea with codeine and that the headache and slight fever after the three hours would respond to aspirin, but Anne was becoming increasingly intrigued about the recurring fevers.

'You can't keep going on like this,' she said for the umpteenth time. 'For goodness sake go to the doctor. If you don't go I'll have to drag you there.'

'I will if it happens again,' said Peter. 'I promise.'

But of course it didn't happen again because he'd solved the problem. To Anne's surprise he suddenly got better.

'I wonder what caused it?' she mused. 'It's a weird condition that comes and goes.'

'I think I'm over it,' said Peter firmly, smiling to himself. After all, he was in control. He'd found the perfect alibi, all he had to do now was plan the perfect murder, and that took him almost another week of concentrated thought.

He knew that Anne went to see her lover regularly, and so he had to be sure that she was going to see him on her usual Thursday.

'Got anything planned for this week?' he asked casually.

'Just the usual. Thought I'd do some painting.'

'On Thursday?'

'Yes, unless you want me for something else. What are you doing?'

'I'll be at the Institute,' he lied.

On that fateful Thursday Anne cooked breakfast and Peter set off to the station at his usual time. The weather forecast was for heavy rain, ideal for an apparent slip into the canal. In Maidenhead he killed time reading a newspaper in a cafe until he was ready, and when his watch showed 8:15, he approached the cafe owner.

'I'm very sorry,' he said. 'But could I use your toilet?'

The man reluctantly agreed.

In the scruffy lean-to in the backyard Peter carefully sucked toxin into a syringe and jammed the needle into his thigh. Then he went back into the cafe, took two codeine tablets, washed them down with another tea and killed time for another half hour. By then he could feel the toxin starting to work, and so he walked quickly to the doctor's surgery where he found four women sitting impatiently in the waiting room. That was good, the delay would make sure that the toxin had had time to work and with luck he would present himself to his GP with a raging fever. To his delight it went exactly to plan.

Dr James looked concerned as he took Peter's pulse and temperature. 'Have you had this before?' he asked.

'Not recently,' lied Peter

'It looks like flu,' continued the doctor. 'But there's been none around this year. And your chest seems clear. I think you should go to the hospital to see what they think.'

That was the last thing Peter wanted. 'I'd rather not,' he said. 'Couldn't I go home and take some aspirin? That usually works. And Anne will be there to keep an eye on me.'

Dr James was doubtful. 'All right then. If you're sure she'll be there. But tell her to call me immediately if you feel worse or the temperature doesn't go down.'

'Thank you Doctor.'

Peter walked carefully back to his house, making sure that he spoke to the man who was cutting the front lawn a few houses down from him. The neighbour looked aghast at Peter's sweating face.

'I've got the flu,' said Peter plaintively. 'I felt ill going to work, so I've come home to bed.'

'Poor old you.'

In the house he threw off his clothes, put extra blankets on the bed and crawled in, setting the alarm for one. Eventually he dozed off, but then he got a telephone call from Deirdre Pearce. He told her irritably that he was too ill to talk and was going to take the telephone off the hook so that he could get some sleep.

In practice he didn't need the alarm. After three hours sleep he felt a little better and went downstairs to rehydrate himself with several glasses of sweet orange juice. Outside it was raining hard. He could feel his energy coming back and felt pleased with himself. The correct dose of toxin had worked like a charm, giving him a short, sharp fever which had fooled the doctor and provided the beginning of his alibi. He took more codeine for his headache and cramping gut, and sat at the kitchen table thinking. Next would be the tricky bit; he had to get out of the house, commit the crime and get back in again without being seen.

He took a long time checking every detail before he went upstairs and took the small suitcase from the wardrobe. In to it went some old jeans, a sweater, some oilskins, a pair of binoculars and a fishing rod and reel. The rod was actually a roach pole which split into seven small sections and so it fitted easily into the case. Finally he added a box of floats and hooks and closed the lid. He made sure the telephone was still off its hook, picked up the case and went out into the garden, where he climbed over the fence, making absolutely sure that no one was watching. Once there he was on a footpath to a neighbouring street and this allowed him to bypass his neighbours. At the station he nodded to the regular ticket clerk, who assumed that he was late and on his way to London, but in reality he took the fast train to Reading. The weather forecast was not correct; it was now sun and showers, and a rainbow hung brilliantly over Reading station as he changed to the stopping train for Woolhampton. He found an empty compartment where he put on jeans and sweater and packed away his suit.

When he arrived the sun was beating down, and the road was steaming as he walked slowly towards the lock. Near the canal he opened his case, took out the fishing paraphernalia and hid the case carefully under a hedge. That done, fisherman Peter cautiously approached the canal, first checking that the MG was in its usual place. It was, and the sight of it made his heart pound and started him sweating again.

The walk had totally exhausted him, and he found a spot by a derelict machinery hut where he could rest and couldn't be seen from the cottage. His head was killing him, but he forced himself to set up his fishing rod and line, and become a lone anonymous angler. Every few minutes he scanned the canal with his binoculars, focusing on the cottage, but there was no sign of Anne or her lover. Suddenly the sun disappeared behind a cloud and a breeze whipped up, and Peter knew he was in for another shower. He put on his oilskins and cowered behind the hut as the rain hurled down. Gradually it eased, and as it did Peter stood up and looked at the cottage. He thought he saw a figure outside the front door, but by the time he wiped the rain of his binoculars it had gone and yet another rainbow hung over the valley. Finally it started to rain really heavily. He looked at his watch; it was five to four, and he packed up his fishing equipment. He knew she'd have to make a move soon, and right on cue she did. Through the binoculars he saw her leave the house and saw the smeared figure of Stuart waving her goodbye. By the time she reached the lock gates it was sheeting down, drumming on the corrugated iron roof of the hut where he waited for her. She saw him for the last time as she stepped off the lock. She opened her mouth to speak, and then she was gone, spinning like a doll into the void, her scream drowned by the hammering of the rain. Peter turned away, feeling hugely tired.

On his slow trudge back he collected his suitcase from the nettles and changed back into his city suit in the gent's at the station. Luckily it was still dry. He left the suitcase on the train, the leather was sodden, and if he had taken it home it would be a sure indication that he'd been out of the house. After that it all went well; by the time he got to Maidenhead the rain had gone and he used his circuitous route to get back to the house without being seen. He was feeling so ill it took a huge effort of will to climb over the fence, but once in the kitchen he felt safe. Just five more things to do.

First. Go to garage, take toxin out of the fridge and inject five milligrams.

Second. Wash syringe carefully, put with other scientific bits.

Third. Take ampoule toxin to bathroom, push round U bend of toilet with hand. Flush toilet, make sure ampoule gone.

Fourth. Put away suit and shoes, get into pyjamas.

Fifth. Set alarm for an hour.

Actually it wasn't the alarm that awoke Peter, but a huge surge of nausea that forced him to run to the bathroom, where he vomited violently into the toilet. As he lay on the floor the room rocked around him and his teeth chattered with fever. He crawled to the telephone in the study, but his hands were shaking so badly that it took three attempts to dial the correct number.

'Surgery, can I help you?'

'I need to speak to Dr James, it's an emergency.'

'And who are you sir?'

'Peter Stott.'

Eventually Dr James came on the line.

'How are you Peter?'

'Pretty dreadful. I'm vomiting, got really bad diarrhoea and a hell of a fever.' His voice trailed off.

'Peter.' The doctor's voice was urgent. 'I need to speak to Anne.'

'She's not home yet.'

'Dear God. Peter, listen carefully. I need you to get the front door and unlock it. Can you do it?'

'I'll try.'

'Hang on in there Peter. I'm on my way.'

Peter inched his way down the stairs on his behind. The banisters were moving like trees in the wind and he thought he could see two figures sitting on the bottom step. They disappeared as he got closer. He unlocked the front door, looked back at the stairs and saw Anne and Michael sitting there smiling at him. He screamed and screamed until he fell unconscious, and he was still unconscious when Dr James found him, lying in a pool of vomit and diarrhoea.

Three hours later the consultant at Reading Hospital was giving his orders to the houseman and nurses.

'This seems to be one of the worst cases of an infected colon that I've seen. Keep on with the ice packs to stop him frying, and keep using them to keep his temperature to about hundred and two. He's on a drip for his dehydration and we'll have to monitor his electrolytes regularly and modify his drip accordingly. And we'll need to keep an eye on his kidneys. We've sent a faecal sample to the lab for culture, but he'll be dead if we wait for the results. So will have to infuse a cocktail of antibiotics and hope one works. All clear? By the way, any news of his wife?'

'No Doctor.'

Peter improved slightly in the small hours of Friday morning, and his condition was officially listed as being "critical but stable". On Saturday he recovered consciousness, but was so weak he could barely speak and he remained almost moribund for another two days. His temperature was down, but not normal. The police turned up to talk to him on Monday, but the doctors said he was too weak for any visitors. The lead policeman at the hospital was actually the newly promoted detective, Ian Johnson, who had been briefed by his superior in Reading police station earlier that day.

'Do you remember Peter Stott, Ian? I think you worked on his case a couple of years back.'

'The scientific detective? Yes, I remember him well.'

'And how did you find him?'

'Likeable,' replied Ian. 'Intelligent, a bit cool, but a real family man.'

'Not any more. His son died of cancer some time back, and his wife apparently drowned accidentally in the Kennet and Avon canal on Thursday.'

'Poor sod,' said Ian sympathetically.

'He could be a bit more than a poor sod,' replied his boss. 'He could just be a jealous husband getting his own back, though I very much doubt it. There could also be a jealous lover. Anyway, that's for you to decide. It's your case, and here's the file.'

Chapter 12
Understanding

Ian's first job was to go to the lock and see the scene of the accident himself. On one lock gate the green slime on the wood just above the water line had been wiped away, and the forensic team had found bits of hair and skin attached to the timber. There was no blood, but then it had been raining hard. He interviewed Anne's lover, and found the man distraught and totally beside himself with grief.

'I'm sorry I have to ask this, Mr Stuart, but how were things between you and her?'

'They were good most of the time. But I didn't like her staying on with her husband, I wanted her to come back to me full-time.'

'And what did she say to that?' asked Ian.

'She said she felt loyalty to Peter for old times' sake. Said she wanted to make amends for things that had happened in the past, whatever that meant. Said she'd come back eventually.' He started sobbing again.

'I'm really sorry, Mr Stuart,' said Ian. The man was either completely innocent or a superb actor. 'I'm sorry to have bothered you at such a time. I'll go now.'

The autopsy said the cause of death was drowning, and that the skin abrasions to the scalp and the bruised shoulder had happened before death. The slime lost from the lock gates coincided with the green stain on Anne's coat, and seemed to indicate that she'd fallen in head first, bumping her shoulder on the lock gate and scraping her head.

Ian returned to the hospital on Saturday afternoon, where the nurses told him that Peter knew of his wife's death and that he was being visited by some colleagues. The detective was intrigued to see Peter being comforted by two attractive women, and he insisted that they leave before starting his interrogation.

'I'm truly sorry at your loss, Dr Stott. But you must realise that we have to clarify the cause of your wife's death, and so I have to ask you a few routine questions.'

Dr Stott nodded, and Ian went in for the kill.

'Do you know John Stuart?'

For a split second he thought he saw recognition in Stott's eyes, but it was quickly followed by denial.

'No, I don't think so. Who is he?

'Your wife's lover.'

This time the correct response. Seemingly genuine shock, denial, and fury, and Ian was virtually convinced of Peter's innocence, but there was still a nagging doubt. His suspect had supposedly been ill in bed all day and in desperate straits that evening. Could he have left the house? He put the question to Peter's consultant, and got a definitive answer.

'Impossible. He had a temperature of 101 when his doctor saw him in the morning, and it was 105 that evening. The fever must have been increasing during the day, and he couldn't possibly have gone out. His symptoms are that of classical bacterial endotoxic poisoning.'

'Did all the tests confirm that, Doctor?'

The consultant looked embarrassed.

'All but one. We did a bacterial culture on his faeces, and expected to find only E. coli there. Strangely enough it was a mixed culture.'

'So what did you make of that?' asked Ian excitedly

'I don't know. The lab must have made a mistake, looked at the wrong culture plate. But there was absolutely no doubt that he had a huge bacterial infection in his gut.'

'So how can you be so sure if the lab culture didn't show it?'

'Because within a few hours of us giving him antibiotics he started to improve, and he kept improving. The antibiotics were obviously killing off the pathogenic bacteria, and they saved his life.'

Ian nodded reluctantly. There was no way he could argue against that. Even if Peter knew of his wife's lover it didn't mean that he was involved. After all, what man likes to admit that he has been cuckolded?

In his private ward, Peter was being consoled by Susan and Deidre Pearce, but had he been present at the conversation between policeman and consultant he would have laughed. He'd tricked them, just as he hoped he would. In reality the antibiotics had not killed off the bacteria which produced the toxin because there were no pathogenic bacteria there to be killed. He had got better because the toxin had been gradually eliminated from his body in the normal way, and all the antibiotics had done was to prevent any further infection in his ulcerated gut.

Peter stayed at Reading Hospital for almost two weeks before he was sent to a convalescent home in Pangbourne for further recuperation. Back at home he managed to cope with the help of a retired nurse who came in to cook his meals, and after a month's absence he was back at work, where he stayed silent and morose. Susan assumed that this was part of the grieving process, but in reality Peter was sick with worry as he waited for the outcome of the inquest. In practice he needn't have worried: all went well, and the coroner recorded a verdict of accidental death and gave his sympathy to Peter and John Stuart, who were both sitting with averted eyes in front of him. Anne's body was then released and started its long and expensive journey to Mull where she was interred next to her father in the drizzle of a Tobermory afternoon. Mum had aged overnight; she was appalled at the manner of her daughter's death and at Anne's obvious betrayal of her marriage. She felt genuinely sorry for Peter, who was in turn generating true guilt over what he'd done to a person who had been such a loving mother substitute to him. He returned to London feeling depressed and sick with guilt.

Peter was ever the pragmatist and knew that hard work usually got him through most crises, and he devised one of the most extensive research programmes of his career. At work he carefully avoided any mention of Anne. Life at Maidenhead was in order; Peter had a lady to clean and prepare his evening meals, a man to keep the garden tidy, and the Institute cafe to give him breakfast, but what he really wanted was peace of mind, and that was not forthcoming.

Christmas came around again and once more Aunt Alice and Susan debated whether to ask Peter up for dinner. Susan asked him tentatively, and received a polite but firm 'no thanks'. His ex-mistress Louise also made contact and he turned her down flat. During the festive season he wanted to be alone at home, when he redesigned a rockery in the garden and fished for pike with huge success.

'How was your Christmas?' asked Susan tentatively.

'It was fine. I wanted to do it solo. And strangely enough I rather enjoyed it.'

'And you didn't miss—your family?' Susan was breaking the taboo on Anne for the first time.

Peter's guard was down, and he answered almost truthfully.

'I didn't miss Anne as much as I missed Michael.'

The conversation stopped instantly, with Susan hardly believing what she had heard and Peter regretting his momentary lapse into honesty. Later, as she reflected on the events of the day she realised delightedly that she was in with a chance. Peter *wasn't* grieving for his dead wife.

Contrary to Anne's continuous suspicions Peter had never really showed any romantic interest in Susan. He had always regarded her as his trusted assistant and fellow colleague, and Anne's sexuality and exuberance had always kept him firmly on the marital straight and narrow. But that was then, things had moved on, and the fact that Susan was interested in him gave him food for thought. He didn't like work liaisons, and above all he didn't want to hurt their excellent working relationship by making a wrong first move. Susan waited in turn; the first move had to come from him.

That move actually came almost six months later and followed an excellent matinee at the Aldwych. Susan had never been to a proper West End theatre before, as she was a movie girl, but Paul Scofield's performance in the Man for All Seasons had her riveted as never before. Peter held her hand for the first time throughout the performance and Susan's nerves were on fire. Then an early supper, and then in the solitude of an empty train compartment he kissed her for the first time. She responded delightedly, but as he became assertive she fought back furiously, both against him and her own rising passion. Their first time together, it had to be *right*, not *here*, not in a scruffy compartment filled with litter and cigarette ends. Peter kept forcing himself on her and finally, in desperation, she kicked him expertly in the groin. He collapsed with a groan, clutching his bruised testicles.

'What was that for?' he roared indignantly, looking up at her. To his surprise she was smiling. She took his face in her hands and kissed him gently on the mouth.

'Peter dear, I'm so sorry. Not here.'

Peter said nothing. His balls were still in agony, and while he remained doubled up, Susan continued cheerfully.

'My dear Dr Stott. I have some good news for you. There is a nice little technician who is dying to be invited for a romantic weekend at some nice hotel in the country. All you have to do is ask her.'

Peter managed a half-hearted grin and nodded. His groin still ached, but he knew he'd been made a good offer. With rising spirits he accompanied Susan back to Ilford.

Next Friday Peter brought the MG to London, and after lunch they set off down the A4 to Bath, where they checked in to the Grosvenor. Susan was shaking with nerves, but everything went well. Their bedroom was lovely, the food excellent and the sex was marvellous. Peter was a skilled and sensitive lover: orgasms were no problem and Susan was in seventh heaven. For the first time in her adult life she was truly happy.

Back at the Institute the news of their affair spread like wildfire and some of the staff were shocked at Peter starting a new relationship so soon after his wife's death, but most staff were happy for them; after all, Anne's behaviour had been atrocious. To be completely circumspect Peter told director Stephens of their affair, and to prevent any conflict of interest, Susan was permanently assigned to work with Deirdre Pearce. She was so happy that she didn't care what anybody thought or who she worked for, and Aunt Alice was also delighted for her.

'Love has certainly brought colour to your cheeks,' she observed. 'You look absolutely marvellous. Peter is obviously good for you.'

As the affair continued they spent most of their weekends away, and occasionally Peter stayed with Susan at Ilford when Alice was absent. Susan didn't want to go to Maidenhead—that was Anne's house, and Peter wasn't sure he wanted her there. That situation existed for months until Susan realised that she'd have to confront her demons and insisted on visiting Peter at home. She assumed that he had got rid of all his wife's possessions and was shocked to find the wardrobe in the main bedroom still filled with Anne's clothes. The studio was also strewn with painting materials and easels, and Peter was sleeping in the spare bedroom.

'Peter,' she said determinedly. 'You can't go on like this. I can't possibly be here with all her stuff around.'

Peter agreed. 'I know,' he said pathetically. 'I've tried to do it, but every time I start I seem to lose my nerve.'

'Do you want me to help?'

'Please.'

'Right,' she said assertively. 'I'll organise things. I'll take a day off on Friday if that's all right with Deirdre, and I'll bring Alice down here to help out. Would that be okay? By the time you get back here in the evening all will be done and you'll get one of her super suppers.'

Peter smiled gratefully and nodded.

That Friday evening it was all finished; Anne's clothes had all gone to the Salvation Army and her jewellery was packed up to be sent to the local auction room. Her old Gallery in Marlow had turned up to collect all the artists' materials and any completed pictures were carefully packed up ready to be sent to Jamieson's in London. The only thing they did forget was the back scullery with its junk, jam jars and pickles, but that didn't matter as it could be dealt with later. Anne's presence in the house had been virtually eliminated and Susan could now happily stay there.

Peter had read in novels that the murderers always return to the scene of the crime, but that didn't stop him going back to the lock on the anniversary of his wife's death. It had been pouring with rain on the day Anne died, but today there was bright afternoon sunshine. The sun was so low in the sky that it blinded him, and down the canal he couldn't see the house where Anne had stayed with her lover. He sat down on a bollard by the lock and looked down. Out of the sun the water was inky, and he shivered, hoping her end had been quick. Then from nowhere came the words.

'You didn't kill her.'

Peter turned, looking straight at the figure which was surrounded by a halo of light. It spoke again, moving forward.

'You didn't do it,' said the female voice.

The figure moved sideways into the shade and her face became clear. *It was Anne.* Peter screamed, falling off the bollard and sliding in terror on his back until his head bumped into a wall. He almost choked as she advanced, and he curled up like a baby, covering his head and moaning in fear. He expected to die, but nothing happened. Instead the figure sat down calmly on the next bollard. He turned his head to try to look at her, then vomited into the lock. She waited till he had finished.

'It's all right,' she said. 'I'm not her, I'm not that cow. Look at me.'

Peter looked up cautiously. The girl was about eighteen, a younger version of Anne, and with the same beautiful eyes. She handed him a bottle of Tizer.

'You'll need to rinse your mouth out,' she said.

Peter did as he was told. He was still shaking violently and couldn't speak, so she answered his unspoken question.

'I'm her daughter,' she said. 'That bitch was my mother.'

Peter could only gape, and the girl continued.

'We were all happy,' she said. 'Mum, Dad and me. They'd always told me I was adopted and it didn't bother me. They loved me and I loved them. Then Mum died when I was thirteen, and it was terrible. But we got through it, Dad and I, and we were happy together until *she* turned up. She thought just because she was my mother that I would be pleased to see her, but I wasn't. I hated her.'

Peter could barely take this all in.

'Your mother,' he croaked. 'Anne?'

'Yes. That blue-eyed slut.'

'Jesus.'

He just lay there, trying to get things straight, while his heart tried to explode out of his chest.

'But how?' he gasped.

'Apparently she got pregnant when she was at the high school on the mainland in Scotland. Her parents made her have me adopted at birth and she never saw me. After her—your son died—she contacted a detective agency and they tracked me down. I didn't like her. I didn't want anything to do with her. Then she took up with Dad, started living with us and I couldn't stand it. I moved out, got a job at a Selfridges in London where they had accommodation for their trainees. When she went back to you Dad moved back here to be close to her, and I only came back to see him occasionally when she wasn't around. She was a two timing bitch, but Dad was so besotted with her he accepted the situation. I tried to keep away.'

Peter could still barely speak. 'And then?'

'Came back that afternoon on the off chance to see Dad, hoping she'd gone. *But she was still there.* I hung around, waiting for her to go. It was raining, and I was soaking wet, and then I saw you.'

There was a long, long silence.

'So you saw what happened,' said Peter carefully. His brain was starting to work.

'Yes, I saw. I was pleased. I wished I'd done it myself. After you'd gone I came over to make sure she was dead.'

Peter said nothing. Surely this nightmare had to stop soon.

'She wasn't. Dad had taught her to swim. She was hanging onto the lock gate when I got there. She could easily have got out.' The girl indicated a rusty ladder at the end of the lock.

Again Peter stayed silent.

'She saw me. Called for help, but I wasn't there for that. I picked up one of those.' She indicated some loose industrial blue bricks lining the edge of the lock. 'I dropped one in on her. It hit her on the shoulder, making her head bang on the lock gate. Then her face went down and she disappeared. I stayed there to make sure it was all over. Then I walked back to the station and went back to London. Actually I think I was on the train after you.'

Events had overtaken Peter's power of speech once again.

'Aren't you glad she's dead?' asked the girl.

The question seared through his brain, and he could barely answer.

'I was,' he said slowly. 'But not now. She was a good mother to Michael.'

'But not to *me*.'

'True. Not to you. I'm sorry. I don't know what to say. I don't even know your name.'

'It's Leonora. And I know yours, Peter. So what now?' She looked at him fiercely. 'Are you glad you didn't kill her?'

'I suppose so.' He hesitated. Realism was returning. 'But your secret's safe with me.'

'I know.' She smiled beautifully, like her mother. 'We are partners in crime.'

'Yes,' said Peter. 'I suppose we are.'

They sat silently for a few minutes, watching the water in the lock turn even blacker.

'I must go,' she said coolly. 'Tea time.' She held out her hand and shook his. 'It's been *so* lovely to meet you at last.'

The situation was so surreal that Peter almost laughed. He watched in disbelief as the young copy of his murdered wife walked slowly over the lock gates and up to the cottage to make tea for her grieving father. She did not look back.

He sat by the lock until it was almost dark. A young boy fisherman, there to catch carp in the twilight, looked at him anxiously.

'You okay mister?'

'Yes,' said Peter. 'I'm fine. Just thinking, getting things straight.'

The boy nodded, and dropped his baited hook into the lock.

Peter's thoughts spun through his head as he drove home, but it was difficult to think clearly because his lower rib cage was tender from all that vomiting. At home he couldn't sleep because his brain was in overdrive, and he stayed awake for hours. Some things were now becoming clear. He understood at last why there had been permanent antipathy between Anne and her mother, and why her father had died early of a broken heart. The illegitimate pregnancy of the daughter of a Presbyterian minister must have been a hugely catastrophic event. He also understood why Anne's mother had expected her daughter to get morning sickness, and he realised that Anne had used the private detectives in Birmingham to track down Leonora. He almost felt sorry for Anne; she had spent months tracking down her daughter, and then, having found her, had been totally rejected. But he still couldn't understand why his wife had returned home to him while she was having an affair with her daughter's adoptive father. That question kept hammering through his head, and it was still unanswered when he finally fell into an exhausted sleep.

Next morning Peter's stomach was still aching, so he had a light breakfast of cornflakes and toast, and began to feel better. Susan was coming around later, and he guiltily remembered that he'd promised to finally clean out those wretched cupboards in the scullery. She had been on at him for days about them, and so he made a start. Inside the first cupboard, with a mass of cooking paraphernalia, he found four large jars of pickles and two unopened glass bottles filled with yellow cooking oil. Both had undecipherable labels in Anne's familiar scrawl. He picked up the pickle jars, put them on the kitchen draining board and opened them. Next he put a colander in the sink and poured the contents of the jars into it, letting the vinegar flow down the drain and collecting the pickles so he could put them in the rubbish. Next he put the bottles of oil on the draining board, and as he did so he bumped one against an empty pickle jar. The bottle cracked, and a gentle stream of oil dribbled down the draining board. In the wet sink the oil formed yellow globules—which turned pink as they made contact with the acidic vinegar around the drain. Peter gaped, and his memories stirred. He took a wineglass from the cupboard, half filled it with water and topped it up with cooking oil. Then he shook the glass holding his hand over the top. The oil and water mixed, then separated, with the oil floating on top and the water underneath. There was a slight yellow tint in the water, and Peter's heart hammered in his chest as he began to understand. He added a few drops of vinegar to the wineglass and shook it again. The water and oil separated as before, but this time the water turned pink, and as it did so he remembered the words of his high school chemistry teacher years ago.

'DAB, dimethylaminoazobenzene, is an easy indicator, Peter. The flask in front of you has got water and DAB in it, so it's yellow. If you add acid it'll turn pink. And then if you neutralise the acid it it'll turn back yellow. *That beautiful colour is why they call it butter yellow.*'

Peter understood it all at last. He knew why Anne had come back to him, and the answer was so obvious that he nearly laughed at his own stupidity. Revenge, the oldest motive in the world. For Michael. With cancer-causing butter yellow. Then the pain grumbling in his stomach suddenly knifed, driving deep under his ribs, and he knew it was the beginning of his end.

Chapter 13
Requiem

Susan was sitting in the garden, luxuriating in the June sun and sipping a glass of milk on what would have been Peter's birthday. The doctor had told her she must keep up her level of calcium and vitamins so that the baby would grow properly. She'd found out that she was pregnant just before Peter became ill, but had delayed telling him until she was absolutely certain. By then he'd received his death sentence, but he was still delighted at her news.

'That's marvellous,' he said. 'Have it. I'll see you right.'

He was as good as his word. Three days later they got married at the registry office in Maidenhead with just Aunt Alice and a bystander as witnesses, and the following day he signed his will leaving everything to Susan.

Peter lived barely three months after he had discovered the butter yellow in the cooking oil. Susan had wanted him to take cytocide, but Peter would have none of it. He knew he was beaten, and wanted to go. He was put on morphine and most of the time sat quietly in his armchair looking out over the river. Unknown to Susan he often thought about Anne, and almost smiled in grudging respect. Touché, my dear. Well played, you really fooled me. Putting the butter yellow in my food and then leaving me was one thing. Coming back as the forgiving wife to finish me off with it was a touch worthy of the Borgias. Bloody brilliant.

Just before the end he gave Susan a letter.

'I want you to open this at noon on my birthday,' he said. 'So you'll remember me.'

Susan burst into tears.

His end was not as bad as she had anticipated. He went into a coma and remained unconscious for a week until his breathing stopped. No blood, no vomit, almost no change. It was just that the gaunt figure in the bed was no longer moving. The certificate said that cause of death was primary carcinoma of the liver.

His funeral was well attended. He had been a popular member of the staff at MICR, and almost all his colleagues turned out to see him off. Deirdre Pearce and Aunt Alice were in floods of tears. Everyone there thought it ironic and tragic that he died of the disease which he had tried to cure in humans and had induced many times in animals. None of them in their wildest dreams imagined that the disease had been induced in him, and Peter kept his secret to the grave.

The church clock chimed twelve and Susan picked up the envelope, which was small and sealed down with red sealing wax. She opened it cautiously. Inside was a photograph of Peter, standing by the river with his late son in his arms, and on the back were just seven words in his familiar capitals.

HAVE A BOY AND CALL HIM MICHAEL